Hannah Crow is in her early thirties and lives in Cornwall.

'Impressively captures the authentic stink of modern England – that hidden world of Fred West, Stephen Lawrence killers and child porn – and the reader is caught up in the texture and decay of contemporary urban life. Crow's not-unreasonable view is that abuse renews itself from generation to generation in geometrical progression, unless the cycle is broken by the redemptive power of love. So Lee is rescued by his friendship with an outrageously camp homosexual, before fully rediscovering his humanity by falling for a "fat bird". Harrowing at times, but deeply thought-provoking nevertheless'   *BIG ISSUE*

'Lee's cool, deadpan voice offers a witty and profoundly disturbing glimpse of a particular brand of male working-class culture . . . a distinctive and compassionate debut'

CHRISTINA PATTERSON, *OBSERVER*

LEE TREBILCOCK IN THE TWENTIETH CENTURY

Hannah Crow

TRANSWORLD PUBLISHERS
61–63 Uxbridge Road, London W5 5SA
a division of The Random House Group Ltd

RANDOM HOUSE AUSTRALIA (PTY) LTD
20 Alfred Street, Milsons Point, Sydney,
New South Wales 2061, Australia

RANDOM HOUSE NEW ZEALAND
18 Poland Road, Glenfield, Auckland 10, New Zealand

RANDOM HOUSE (PTY) LTD
Endulini, 5a Jubilee Road, Parktown 2193, South Africa

This paperback edition published 2000 by Anchor,
a division of Transworld Publishers

First published in Great Britain by Anchor, 1999

10 9 8 7 6 5 4 3 2 1

Copyright © 1999 by Hannah Crow

A catalogue record for this book is available from the British Library

ISBN 1862 30080 1

Typeset in Adobe Caslon by Kestrel Data, Exeter, Devon
Printed and bound in Great Britain by
Mackays of Chatham plc, Chatham, Kent

The bottle was filled with passion and love just as young poets are before they know much about either.

Hans Christian Andersen,
The Bottle

Contents

1. Lorraine Gets Her Menstruation

I was a floor operative in a do-it-yourself multichain. I was nineteen. I was a kid and I liked it. I spoke in short sentences when the need arose and I rolled my own smokes. I played the birds like a virtuoso strumming the bridge off a Stradivarius.

I wouldn't have chosen floor operative if we'd all had the choice in life. I would have chosen bank clerk or one of those middle-class occupations but I never got around to it. Too busy strumming when I should have been learning.

I wore a lime-green operative's romper with my name embossed into a cream acrylic oblong badge on my chest. L-E-E. Like so. I had the badge attached to my white T-shirt through the breast pocket of the romper so the pin would act to prevent my undergarment curling and riding when I was lifting and bending. It was a tip I got from Lorraine, assembled kitchens.

Before I started hanging around Lorraine in my breaks, I was forever pulling and tugging through the hole in the base of the romper to refix the T-shirt. Apart from the T-shirt and romper I was completely naked except for pants, socks and black comfortable shoes with rubber soles. Comfortable shoes made me uncomfortable – I was nineteen, it was normal – so I wore the romper at full mast without the supplied waist belt so that if anyone I knew came by, they would have to look for the shoes among the slack material. Although the people I knew were capable of looking and distracting until they found, I deliberately kept things brief in those situations.

Lorraine Sweet worked at the Do It Easy and most nights before I snapped on my bedside Awakener, I wished she did do it easy.

She was older. She smoked menthol cigarettes and had an ex-husband. She touched my arse once when I was lunging for a ready pack of two-by-four in dispatch. I nearly dropped the lot on to my comfortable shoe and then I wouldn't have been so comfy. Instead I reached round and grabbed at her because that's my instinct as a male. A bird won't reach to grab you because she thinks you're attacking her but a lad will reach to grab on and enjoy. I reached to grab on and enjoy but Ronald my supervisor was advancing around the corner whistling the signature to 'The Liverbirds' television programme and I knew it wasn't worth it since his wife frequently visited Lorraine at home to measure for curtains. Ronald's wife worked in tailored-to-fit thermal linings and she and Lorraine had struck up a friendship. I stroked Lorraine's little finger while she was demonstrating one of our kitchens – Distressed Aplomb Urban Architecture in display four – and she had acted as if she hadn't noticed and asked me to go and select a water-based undercoat in Frenzy shade. I knew the run of the birds and knew exactly what she meant and went to paints to wait for her but she must have got held up.

Lorraine liked to read the paper at lunchtime in the staff canteen with her arm along the top of the microwave. She always read the problem page out loud and it often involved a delicate situation with a young boy and an older woman in the workplace. I think she made them up because one time I picked up the paper when she had gone outside to the skips with her menthols and orange sports lighter and there was only a small piece from a bird with thrush, a real bird I mean not an animal, and a bloke whose bird was running amok in a small town with all the married blokes so that everyone knew and what should he do. So I was sure she was trying to say something but that she was shy. She was pretty sexy anyway, Lorraine, and she spoke with a low voice that sort of climbed its way out of her larynx and paused for a split second to marvel at the wonder of a palate and set of teeth. Actually two of the teeth were false from a donkey-riding beach accident. She told me.

There she would be, straining out of her flower-embroidered blouson and sleeveless cardigan, running her fingers over the defrost knob, and all the while I would be finding it hard to position the company newsletter over my lap and growing groin. There was little support in the lime-green romper and I reckon Lorraine knew that. Morgan, the lad on the customer services till, said she had offered him oral satisfaction when they were going through the throes of a sweet and sour Pot Goddess micro-meal in the canteen but he turned her down because he couldn't risk disease which I thought was a bit unfair on Lorraine but probably true.

The Day It Started

The day it started I clocked on at eight fifty-nine. I put my stiff beige card into the timer slot and punched. I always put my time card at the top of the slim holder because I knew Lorraine liked to be under whoever was at the top. It was a game we played. I'd got rid of Morgan from the top when Morgan had started going out with Claire in personnel & wages. I didn't mind Claire and if Morgan hadn't got in there, I might have had a recreational crack myself. Claire was slim but washed-out. None of her external parts attracted attention or looked like they needed any sort of administering whereas Lorraine was making pheromones faster than any hormone-replacement plant. Lorraine breathed and you were reaching for the after-fag. Christ at times I just wanted to get my forefinger up the rim of that skirt to find the nylon underwear that I knew would already be sticking together. It didn't bear thinking about. Anyway I didn't or I hadn't as yet.

Morgan and Claire were a happy couple, he waiting for her to run her hand over the dust on the filing cabinet from the morning, she waiting for him to get out of his romper and join her on the lino for home time. If Claire had been the last bird on earth and it had been my job to refit the world with humans, I'd've done the job. Claire wasn't un-attractive with her pale brown eyes and pale brown hair. She just wasn't very enthusiastic and these sallow-skinned birds often tended to pull your dick very hard for some reason and some were bloody demanding, shouting what they wanted and when. I reckoned Lorraine would just sigh a lot and squirm and then start to pant in a ladylike manner until she was pulling the hair out of your crown and then she would arch her back and express a great relief. I loved sex.

After clocking on, I made the point as always of walking

up through kitchens to get to the flapping plastic curtain we worked through. Lorraine was in display two with her back to me, arranging plastic tulips into one of our complementary shade vases. Lorraine had long, manicured nails which meant people often had to do things for her but she arranged beautifully. Her nails were one of the things that made me think she wouldn't be likely to pull my dick off. Women with nails were normally a bit more careful. Their nails put them one step removed from life and me — a step I wouldn't mind taking. Anyway she was very sensitive, Lorraine, and she turned round as I came up alongside tucking my T-shirt into my pants through the unzipped romper.

—Morning, big boy, she said, with a running joke we had.

—Hallo, sex, I responded. Lorraine often flirted with the lads.

—Taking me out tonight, then?

—Sure. Anywhere you say, darlin'. I liked to drop the 'g' with Lorraine.

—Anywhere I want?

—Any way you want.

—I might just take you up on that.

—Take me up? I'd be obliged if you would.

—You're a naughty boy, Lee Trebilcock. You'll cop it one of these days.

—Yeah, promises, sweet Lorraine. I'll cop it with you. You won't want any other cop when you cop it with me.

—You cheeky boy. I've got a son nearly your age.

—Does he know you're out alone?

—I'll bring him in one day. He's got cerebral palsy. He's a super boy. He'd really look up to you, Lee.

—Everyone looks up to me. You could, Lorraine. I mean, I could stroke your ears while you look up to me. Thing is, you'd have your mouth full.

—You're a naughty boy.

—You bet.

I knew Lorraine and I would continue our conversation later so I mooched my way on in the comfortable shoes, giving my groin an encouraging rub on the way. Things around my groin got disarranged when I was near Lorraine and I often had to put them back in the right place. I liked her to know I was putting the two together – her face, my groin.

Ronald was in the yard. I gave him a nod and went towards a stack of boxed heavy-duty multi-glue that needed to go out on the floor. I made a start slashing away at the brown sticky package tape with the camping penknife I liked to wear round my neck on a cord. The knife was a present from a bird in Torquay the Easter I went teen tenting with Hawley. That was before I knew about Hawley and he had ended up sleeping outside the tent every night so I could get the birds in. As it turned out, I lost my cherry on the first night in Torquay at the under-16s disco with a girl called Sherry from Berwick-on-Tweed. She was sixteen but I was a big boy for my age. She took me out the back of the disco hall to where they keep the used soda siphons, which turned out to be the yard of her two-star hotel near the sea front, and she sort of kissed me without tongues and then just grabbed at my dick through my jeans and pants. I think my eyes got wider or at least my pupils because I could suddenly see better what she was up to and she was getting herself ready with a bit of finger work and the lip of a Diet Coke bottle. That was in the days when Coke bottles were long and twisty and handy-sized. Well, I thought, she's been here before. I was interested as much as anything else. The only near-nude woman I'd seen was my old lady in her big bra taking a crap on the toilet bowl the day I hid down the back of the broken spin-dryer. Although one time, when my Aunt Margot was pregnant with Ferd, she'd got me to suck on her nipples to get the milk going, but I wasn't happy.

Well, Sherry was going on like this for a while with her pulling me off and doing herself at the same time and then somehow she got it in. She was an experienced girl and she managed it. I came within seconds. I didn't know what else you were supposed to do but it was good and I saw her the next night for the mother and daughter look-alike contest they were running in the hotel. Hawley and I came in on the bus from the campsite. Hawley was arm-in-arm with a skinny kid from Wrexham called Hugh. I should have known it at the time with Hawley but I didn't think of it. Sherry and I got at it again in her room and she showed me some more tricks and her old dear's sexual aids. She had some apricot brandy her old dear liked to drink before bed to help her sleep.

Sherry gave me the knife on the third day. She said she'd shop-lifted it from the gift shop in the hotel foyer and it was a cracker – corkscrew, pliers, saw, two blades, bottle opener. The front slid off to make a fork and the back slid off to make a knife. She gave me the belt off her towelling beach robe to put it round my neck and I always wore it after that. She got it engraved with one pound fifty from her mother's bedside cabinet. L-E-E. Like so. That was six years ago but the birds loved finding it in my under-garments especially if it was light where we were doing it.

When I'd got the glue all free I put it in one of the trolleys and went to the aisle to stack it away. I was generally in shelving but I might step into adhesives if Simon was bogged down with a delivery which he was. We'd had a recent tragedy in adhesives where some super-strength resin had come away from its wrapper and a couple of identical toddler twins had got themselves stuck together. We had to call the police and everything and they got taken to hospital to get separated. I had to keep them quiet while they sedated the mother on one of the bulk-goods mini-trailers. I basically did Bugs Bunny and all the characters in the Wacky Races cartoon including my favourite, Penelope Pitstop, before going on to the Flintstones. Eventually the tots smiled just as the ambulance took them off squeezed into an adult's wheelchair. The upshot was the mother sued Pete the manager and now adhesives had been taken over solely by 22-year-old scout leader Simon for customer safety. As I'd been there with the toddlers all the way, I was considered responsible enough to deputize for Simon. Plus I'd got two extra gold stars on my name badge which meant that I was halfway to an hourly wage increase which I liked.

I liked being in adhesives. Shelving was boring, mostly do-it-yourself weekenders wanting to put up a phone ledge or kitchen utensils bar. I didn't mind chatting with the lads that got in there for their hardboard, MDF and curly iron wall-brackets but there wasn't the female angle to go for. You might get the odd lesbian in on her day off wanting advice on screw length. I was tolerant of lesbians what with Hawley but I preferred some stimulus in my workday. Now, in adhesives I could get this stimulus. Not only did I have the young mums after paper paste for their kids and rubber glue for their carpet underlay but there was all manner of demand for epoxies, self-bonders, plastic wood, chemical metals, solvents and thinners, in fact it was quite amazing just what these birds did with their glue. And they always needed advice, what would take what, and I was happy to oblige, using 'madam' with the older ones which I could tell they liked. I ran a good department when Simon was answering the phone for Pete and added to that I got a full view of Lorraine's pencil skirt up against the Formica of her kitchen installations. Because from adhesives, kitchens was the department that ran along the back wall. So you could stand pricing or stacking and stare straight ahead without Ronald or anyone knowing any different. Not that Ronald would know anyway. He collected train signs, platform segments and hopper timetables.

Lorraine was nicely placed as I stacked the glues, taking care to keep to the sale price of our Best Buy Of The Week promotion. I stood immediately facing her and looked up and down from my pricing gun. She was with a customer, a middle-aged woman, and she was showing the magnetic catch and opening action of the overhead cupboards, a standard feature of all the kitchens. They were exchanging pleasantries. Lorraine was a good saleswoman, you could tell. You could trust her. If she said she'd have it herself, you felt sure you wanted it and that went for more than just her kitchen displays. The customer was writing down prices and dimensions on to a piece of paper, looking up every now and again to nod. Lorraine had her red file out and was running down the prices with her biro. I got through the first box and slashed free the next on my trolley, slipping my knife back to my chest through my romper neck-gap. Lorraine looked up as I was patting the zip back down and she smiled, mouthing something I didn't catch. She went back to her customer and, the job done, I went to make myself available to Ronald in the back. I liked to be cheery, that was partly how I got the opening in adhesives in the first place.

Morgan needed me in customer services. A sack of sand cement had got damp in dry building and stuck itself to the store shelf. I volunteered to help and made my way along with my hammer drill which I used on these rare occasions. I plugged in to the extension lead I was unwinding under my arm, selected a weighty masonry bit and switched on. It didn't take long to get through the paper and cement and with a few goes the lump finally shifted and it was lunch-time.

Lorraine caught up with me on the way to the canteen, carrying her daily paper in her black soft leather handbag. She had been running and was puffing slightly. I told her she'd wear herself out. She took up her position on the sideboard next to the microwave, parting her legs a little to let the natural fall of her thighs take up the skirt. She wriggled down until we were both comfortable then took up her sandwich box and took out raisin sandwiches. I took out cucumber spread and cheddar cheese. I made my way through two grapefruits, a bag of crisps shaped like monsters' mouths, a bar of nutty chocolate and a pork pie before either of us spoke. Ronald joined us with his weekly special interest magazine, showing us pictures of rail track discarded for use on the Channel Tunnel due to heat-sensitive properties. Lorraine and I expressed a polite interest and then she read out the problem page.

—It says here there's a lad in Bolton who's got himself in a state over a Christmas works fling he's had with an older woman. What about that, then?

I could tell she wasn't talking to Ronald.

—Lucky twat.

Lorraine leaned forward to embrace the microwave.

—Karenza says it's only natural for a young boy to be attracted to an older woman if he's in contact with her day in, day out. What do you think, Lee?

—Day in, day out. Nice. I started on a chocolate chip muffin I'd got out of the freezer the night before.

—Sign of the times, grunted Ronald without looking up. He had a slice of pickled gherkin balanced on his leather hot-cross cardigan button.

—What would you do, Lee?

—What, in that rare situation? I grinned. I'd make sure I gave her one at least that regular. I spoke quietly so as not to disturb Ronald but I knew Lorraine had heard as she stretched out on the sticky microwave top.

—I've got a son nearly your age, she said for the second time that day. I'd heard all about her son. He had cerebral palsy and she took him to the dry-ski slope once a Sunday for a special class.

—Does he like older women?

—No. He's got cerebral palsy.

—It's a shame about your Ray, Ronald chirped. Boy like that needs a father.

—His father joined an oil rig, said Lorraine but we all knew he'd disappeared with the female controller at his classic car hire workplace.

—My old man run out on my old dear, I volunteered. Went out for a packet of twenty Weights in 1983 and never came back. Doctors reckoned that's how my old dear got the baskets.

—You poor boy, said Lorraine genuinely. That was what I liked about Lorraine. She wasn't just a bird in a skirt. She was like your best friend's mother. Well, she wasn't like Hawley's mother because Hawley's mother was bonkers. Lorraine was like your ideal best friend's ideal mother – young, good-looking, understanding and available. I gave her a wink to show I was OK and she finished with blackberry yoghurt where you put the fruits in yourself. Together we went outside with our fag tins and I smoked a roll-up while she lit and sucked on a menthol. Then she went into the Ladies with her handbag and I hung around the noticeboards reading all about childcare.

I had never previously shown an interest in the company

five-a-side hockey team or holiday cottage rental in Anglesey but I found myself scanning the leaflets from the heart council telling you to stop smoking or die and when I'd finished that, I made a start on Ronald's notice for railway enthusiasts to come together and share once a week. I was pressing the furry board with my finger and stuffing hepatitis B leaflets down my romper neck opening when I heard Lorraine's voice from the toilets.

—Lee?

How did she know I was out there?

—Is that you?

—Yeah.

—I've got my hair caught in my love-heart chain at the back. Would you come in and help me?

—What – now? I asked excitedly and for no reason.

—Yes. Now.

—Coming, I said and pushed the Ladies door open with my elbow.

Inside it was bright and clean. There were bits of torn toilet roll on the floor and in the corner there was a bin of ball-shaped paper hand towels. Lorraine had her handbag open on the pink sink ledge and she had some bits of make-up lying out, her Handy Candy lipstick for one. She was standing in front of the mirror so that when I entered she could only see my face in the glass. She had one arm twisted behind her, up at her neck and she was fiddling with her hair.

—Here – if you could just hold my hair up, she said and I went to take it in my hand. Lorraine's dark brown hair was styled into a stiff hairspray shoulder-length cut. I put my right hand over her fingers to feel for the hair and she moved her hand away to fiddle with the catch on the gold neck chain. Within seconds, the chain was free. I went to move my hand but she told me not to. Instead she leant her head back against my free arm and lifted both her hands to circle what I knew to be her nipples. I steeled my arm against her as she lay almost vertically on me.

—You'd better lock that door in case someone comes in.

I locked the door.

—Have you ever done it with an older woman?

—Yes, I said, thinking of Sherry from Berwick-on-Tweed. She was sixteen, I was thirteen.

—No. I mean an *older* woman. A woman like me. She gasped as her buttocks divided themselves around my left arm. She began to rub up and down, forcing her buttocks apart.

—I was a very good dancer when I was young. She raised and lowered on her heels. I could have been in Pan's People.

I still had her hair in my right hand. I was hot under my romper.

—Do you know what happens if I turn round?

—Yes.

—Naughty boy. I can see you've done this before.

—Yes, I said and I had.

I left her hair and put my hand along the hem of her pencil skirt. She stood still, panting slightly, buttocks clenching my left arm. I lifted the skirt as far as her sleeveless cardigan would allow and that was enough to find the nylon suspender belt and suspender tops. She was wearing the suspender belt inside the knickers which she must have enjoyed. The knickers were wrapped over her bottom, held to the skin by fine elastic. They were inexpensive knickers from an inexpensive lingerie collection, I'd seen enough pairs of women's underpants to know. She loosened her tank top cardigan and parted her legs, bending forward and finally freeing my left arm. With both hands now available, I whipped her skirt up and clung to the tops of her thighs at the front, bringing her arse very close to my groin. She reached around with her hands and cupped my head, stroking my facial sideboards. We simulated sex for a while with her holding on to the pink sink ledge with one hand. Then I made bold and got my forefinger into the knickers. I felt Lorraine tense at this moment and she leant forward, reaching into her handbag. As I took a step backward and rubbed her buttocks, she handed round a tube of jelly.

—Use this, Lee.

It was a tube of lubricant. I paused for a second and then, not having used it before, squeezed enough jelly to cover a gum ulcer and used my other hand to pull the knicker gusset aside and get the jelly on. Once the knickers were anchored by one lip to the side of Lorraine's cunt, I was able to work the jelly into her which she enjoyed as she tried to sit on my hand.

—Use more.

I got some more on so that I could easily rub up and down at her arse with a couple of fingers in place to keep me erect. She began panting heavily.

—Can you get your cock out?

I did this, unzipping the length of my romper.

—Is it ready?

I could tell she was, so I said yes and pulled my pants down so I could get it in place. Once at the entrance, I pushed the hilt of my dick up against her until it hurt trying to get it in. Lorraine suggested more jelly and I moved away, noticing thick liquid on my dick. Lorraine was menstruating.

—You're bleeding, Lorraine.

—It's my time, you bastard, she gasped excitedly and I put more jelly on her cunt.

This time I got in and she moved around on it enough to get her going. I was worried about the blood plus I didn't have a Matey One but it was too late now. Lorraine moved her cunt on and off my dick getting faster and soon she was slipping on and off very quickly, sometimes missing altogether. I stood with my legs slightly apart and knees bent to weather her strokes and I leant my head back. I began to get the first throes of orgasm and clutched Lorraine's hips to get her in the right place and speed. She gave up to my force and enjoyed being pulled on and off as I shunted in and out until I held her on if for one long minute and groaned several times to let her know I'd finished.

There was a knock at the door. Claire needed to go to the toilet please. Lorraine swallowed and said she wouldn't be a moment. Claire asked why the door was locked and Lorraine said she was changing. She didn't stop moving and got straight back into it as Claire walked away. I put my right hand around to Lorraine's front and held on there to help things along as well as putting a couple of my left-hand fingers into her since my dick was now soft. She wriggled and moved, forcing until eventually she was calm against the sideboard. I removed my fingers and trailed a strip of red mucus from her cunt into one of the sinks. I washed my hands and bent down to tissue up the other fronds of red fluid that were on the floor. She did her face and we got our clothing back on. She said I'd better go and she would see me later. I unlocked the door and slipped unseen past the back of Claire at the fire extinguisher.

And Then I Saw Her

And then I saw her.

She was standing looking at the large sheets of glue-joined pine we sold in vast quantities. She had taken a sheet out and put it up beside the securing chain and she was holding it towards her, looking down its length. I knew what the bird was doing. She was checking to see that the wood was straight. We'd had a lot of cheap stock in that was rain-damaged and twisted. I stopped to look for a second or two to breathe normally again. She was a funny bird I could see and that wasn't just because she weighed over twenty stone.

She was wearing a short silk bomber jacket over a wide skirt and round her neck she wore a college scarf. She wore gloves with no fingers and thick, pink-rimmed glasses. She was concentrating so hard she didn't notice me as I made my way over. She stepped back and nearly crushed my comfy shoe.

—Oh, I'm sorry, said the bird and she looked down to avoid my eyes.

—That's all right, I said chirpily and helped her with her sheet of wood. Did you want this one?

—Yes, I do. Do you have anything thicker?

I looked at the bird carefully.

—I'll go and have a look.

It was stock I would be putting out that afternoon. It was very heavy and tricky to move so that I would need Ronald's drive-on trolley for the job but I carried the eight-foot slab on my back to where the bird was, putting it down and puffing.

—Oh, how kind, the bird said.

—I'll take it to Morgan at the cash desk for you, I said and together we went slowly over to customer services.

2. Down My Road

I lived in a council house next to a park in a cul-de-sac in south coastal Chivermouth. I had a friend who was a homosexual, an uncle who could get you anything and an old dear with Alzheimer's. I went clubbing, met birds, read car mags and wanked in bed on a Sunday morning before the sheets got changed.

I went to work on Monday morning and came back on Monday evening. I helped the birds with their matt emulsion colour charts and the lads with their nail lengths. I was a tom-cat with the birds and I never wore second-hand clothes. I was the only kid. My old man went missing when I was six. I was crouched on the settee with my pyjamas tucked in waiting for him to get back.

I was a good-looking lad. I had thick furry brown sideboards which hid the spots and tough skin made for the razor blade. I was shaving at fourteen and had my pubic hair off at twelve. I had man's skin and brown eyes like friendly peanuts. I had thin lips and a gap in my teeth for forcing my tongue through when I needed. I had a lean body with a veiny neck, strong chest and flexible legs. I had a rounded white arse and a big dick. I pressed my own shirts for the weekend and I was back by twelve a.m. if it looked like the old dear had forgotten her name.

There was only one of me. I never found out where the old man went nor did the old dear. He went out one day and never came back. I looked out for him through the front window but he never came. We told the police. I was a kid. My Uncle Septor came over the road. He printed up signs of a man in a Swedish logger's hat that clipped monkey-ears under the chin when it was freezing. The man looked surly in the thick photocopy ink. He didn't look like my old man. I was still trying to jump on the old man's lap and get near his wide chest when he went. I wasn't a pathetic kid. I was the only one.

My Old Man

My old man was a Chivermouth man which meant he had a different accent from the rest of the county. He said 'buo-y' instead of 'boy'. The last time I saw him he was in a brown short-sleeve shirt that showed his white vest through. He'd changed after work drilling up the road. He'd had me on his knee. I'd smelt the Fairy soap under his fingernails and felt the hard stubble on his chin. He'd had me curled on his knee in the TV chair so I could see his dark hair curling on to his white and red face. He'd patted the night nappy I wore so I didn't shit in the bed. He'd been telling the old dear about the repairs on the roundabout by the Chivermouth bypass. He'd told her through the serving hatch. I'd stood on his knee with my arm on his shoulder, king of the TV chair castle. I'd talked in French and made the fucking language up and he'd laughed at me. I'd held his forehead with one hand like a kid who holds the high climbing-frame bar when he knows he can go up or down.

He'd put me down by the waist and got out his change from his brown trouser pocket and he'd given me a ten pence and said he needed his fags and I couldn't go. He'd put me on the poof and shouted in to the old dear with her oven-top deep fryer. The old dear hadn't come out. He'd gone out through the door and I'd lain along the settee arching my back, waiting for him to get back to listen to me. He didn't get back and the old dear put the fish bites in the garden for the birds and called my Uncle Septor on the phone and my Uncle Septor came over and sat with her on the settee while she cried 'Frank!' and I went upstairs and tried the razor on the polystyrene wall-covering and wheeled my little Ferrari car over the carpet floor marks where the bed had been moved. I didn't look out of the window and we didn't have curtains.

My old dear was Wendy. She came from the other side of the river which meant she was from another county. She was a dairymaid in an organic cheese farm until it closed. No-one wanted organic cheese in 1976. She moved to Chivermouth to work in a bakery piping jam into doughnuts and sticking Smartie heads on to cup cakes. The old man met her when he went in for cheese and potato slice elevenses when he wasn't drilling up the road. She got pregnant with me and they got a council house on the Surrey Housing Estate. We got the end house before the park where the castle stood in another time. It was two up and two down. We had a slope at the front with slimy stones and dead leaves and a small garden at the back for playing and crapping dogs. The windows were wide, without double-glazing. My old dear wanted double-glazing from the company where you got a free patio door with every set of four frames. Instead she got me. I was early and came out blue. The old man was on the bypass roundabout laying a sleeping policeman after a kid got knocked down and killed. He came to the hospital at the end of the day and looked in at me lying there. She told me.

My old dear was sane in a marriage of inconvenience for seven years until my old man got a mystery appointment with a packet of fags and she took a walk only she never really moved from the spot and I got older just like that. The doctors said they couldn't understand anyone going at thirty-nine like that. I said I could. And she could get incontinent.

Down My Road

There were fifty or so houses up and down my road and the rest of the estate went on around the top of the park. The first twenty houses were the same – two windows on the top and two windows on the bottom. The houses were newer and replaced the prefab bungalows put up in the 1950s for the old folk. The old folk lived in a one-level home of their own round the corner and it was better that way because we didn't see them and we were young.

The houses at the bottom were painted grey and hung with special all-year tiles that let the weather in. The tiles weren't made of slate, they were made of clay with holes in. When the tiles dropped off you could see the holes under the grey paint. The houses stained with rain and crapper overflow. There were built-on green window boxes on the upstairs windows but no-one maintained them. It was difficult to garden them because the windows only opened at the top and we weren't getting the ladders out. Nobody used the window boxes and some burnt them off with small blow torch tins.

Most people bought their houses off the council. My old dear had wanted to buy ours but now she had to wait until I was ready. Our house was at the bottom. It was down a slight slope of three or so feet. You could see into the lounge from the pavement. You could almost see into the front bedroom which was the old dear's. The old dear had the master bedroom. I should have had it really but I didn't want people knowing about the Daffy Duck curtains or the newspaper cut-outs of the topless birds in shiny boots. Inside the front door was the stairs which didn't have any carpet. Uncle Septor laid the runner and lost the deep shag to damp in the lock-up. You walked straight ahead for the kitchen which was a small room leading to the back door. We had a deep freeze in the kitchen, radio cassette, electric kettle, microwave for Pot Goddess meals, hooks for cups, checked Formica tops, boxes of Shreddies breakfast cereal. Out of the kitchen you got into the garden which was grass and a whirligig washing line. No-one used the garden except the estate cats that got everywhere.

If you turned right after the front door you walked into the lounge which was the main room of the ground floor. In the lounge was a stack of put-you-up Regency-style shelves from the Do It Easy, damaged stock, and the old dear had a glass cabinet from her old dear. The old dear's glass cabinet had glass shelves and it was lit by two light bulbs inside so it always had to be near a wall socket. The old dear used to put coloured bulbs in to brighten up the china cart-horses when I was a kid. Now she kept a plastic Eiffel Tower, a slate engraved with a black woodpecker, little sherry glasses with grapes on them, the phone books and a Welsh doll dressed in a black top hat from her honeymoon in Newport.

There were pictures on the lounge walls – the head of a Spanish bird and a famous hay cart. We had a long brown vinyl settee which dragged you back into it and you could sometimes find a few pence down the back of the foam after anyone visited. We had a wooden mantelpiece over the coal fire and the mantel lit up when the fire was switched on. The red light circulated around the coals and the plastic cover was cracked so it let real light through in one place. The old dear's dolls were on the mantelpiece – a Greek bloke in a stiff white kilt, a Czechoslovakian with sticks under her arm and a Red Indian in a chamois leather tunic for attracting the squaws.

Upstairs in the master bedroom the old dear's bed took up most of the room and made it look old. It was a big bed with shiny wood stuck on to the headboard and the old dear had her crochet blankets and cardigans over it. She had a big hairbrush on a dresser which had tapestry under glass on it.

The old dear had built-in white wardrobes like Sindy doll house furniture. Hawley got out his Sindys one afternoon after I met him and I saw what Sindy's house was like. I took my couple of dumper trucks and hawk-eye Action Man round and we played life on the kerb. Hawley had Sindy in a purple roller-skating outfit. Action Man was in a deep red casual sweater and beige easy trousers with pockets on the thigh. Action Man only had one foot so he couldn't use the roller skates but he didn't fucking want to anyway. I wasn't using toys at twelve. I was forging Wendy Trebilcock's child benefit book and smoking herbal tobacco on Nut Avenue.

After our house was the park. The park was big enough for a Sunday morning recreational football game and it had four or so squares of bouncy specialized safety tarmac for kiddies' toys. The older kids generally used the toys and the young ones hung round the benches leaning their forearms along the wood, watching us. Nearest the pitch there was a semi-circle of decreasing-length telegraph poles made into a Red Indian lookout. The middle was an earth gash rubbed to mud where wet formed after spit and rain. The bike treads drove channels into the gash while the cowboys came over the brow of the hill in leather chaps on too-small white and brown ponies to shoot up the sky.

There was a set of three big swings made of car tyres and the older kids jumped on and off them and scuffed up the grass while the dogs pissed down their own legs. The dogs weren't supposed to run free and there was always peaky shit sticking to the pooper shovel sign. Some of the dogs on the estate shat bigger than a man, especially the so-called dangerous dogs. As far as I could see the only dangerous thing about those dogs was if you opened your mouth under their arses when they were taking a crap and that was dangerous. We'd only had one baby death from aggressive German shepherds and we'd had two cases of Jack Russell toxic poisoning.

There was a set of toddler swings but the older kids got on them too, standing up on the stout red plastic frames that held you in if you were five or so. The older kids pushed hard on their knees to make them go faster or else wrapped the swings right round the top pole so no-one else could get them.

There were two plastic-saddled chickens on big springs so that when you got on you could bounce around and bend them over to the floor only the kids ruined them by bouncing too much and the spring got weak and the chickens just hung to one side so they got kicked. The rest of the park was small slopes of grassy castle remains and scrub flower beds. Then you got to the road and Richard's Hair Office and the Pizza Warehouse.

At the top of the road we had Chubby's. Chubby served chips in cones and scampi in yellow polystyrene boxes. He sold butcher's pies in paper bags and cola in see-through cans with straws stuck to the sides with glue. If you didn't have the money you took the chips and came back the next day. Chubby knew everyone. The school kids used to get up to Chubby's and take their newspaper wrappers into the park and they swung on the swings and left paper on the grass and the council environmental officer threatened to close Chubby down so Chubby went into cones which weren't such a mess and he stayed open. Chubby's son, Little Chubby Junior, was fat and he had been in my class and he was a little criminal. He set fire to Chubby's one afternoon with a box of safety matches and a biscuit tin but Chubby didn't report him and he handed the business over to Little Chubby Junior when Little Chubby Junior was eighteen. Now it was Little Chubby Junior behind the stainless steel frying stand, coating cods, pricking sausages and turning chicken quarters. Little Chubby Junior had calmed down a lot but he still had that look in his eye, especially when he was sweeping around on the queuing side. I always nodded to Little Chubby Junior.

The Cars Down My Road

The cars down my road were the types of cars that you knew immediately who drove them even though they weren't remarkable models. Uncle Septor drove a brown Skoda with a red door. It was always parked next to the yellow Fiesta with the travel sweets and tampons on the dashboard. There was a puce rough-terrain four-wheel drive that rarely got out of the cul-de-sac and a khaki Ford Cortina with the back window smashed in so it was freezing in winter. A couple of cars were abandoned due to disinterest. Most of them weren't taxed or they were taxed for a month or so and then the discs got sent back to the tax centre and the money was re-imbursed. Motor insurance was like toilet paper. Nice if you could afford it but if you couldn't you used the *News of the World* or slummed it with bobbly skid marks. Most people down our road were on bobbly skid marks.

Uncle Septor's Skoda drove with cardboard air freshener trees hanging off the rear-view mirror. He had a small axe in the boot and pliers on the back seat. The seats didn't come with the car. They were passed on to him. He had a big wooden dice on the dashboard and the faces were written with 'sex', 'movies', 'drive-in' and so on. When he went out dating he rolled the dice with the bird to see what fate had in store for her. He said it was weighted to sex. It was a present from Richard and Majollica when they went to America to see Elvis's house and they stopped off in Memphis to look at his recording studio. They bought my old dear a tea towel with a deep-fried banana fudges recipe and all Elvis's favourite sweet dishes.

Uncle Septor drove about like a serial killer but he never got stopped. Some parking spaces were just spare parts – wings, bonnets, boots – which had come from other cars, and some cars were being home-sprayed or painted with special paints. You could always see where the spray dribbled and there were paint brush lines too but the way the estate worked was that where something could be done yourself it was stupid not to get on and do it. It meant you could change car colour just like that with a paint brush and a tin of spray paint. So your life had changed and you were in the flow but you'd done it yourself. You were getting the new things everyone else was getting but you were doing it yourself. Like swapping with your neighbour and getting different. Different was new. It stopped all the fights. Every Sunday morning all the bonnets were up and the engines were tweaked and turned over and the boys wandered up and down maintaining the cars like they were a communal fleet and they were.

The main thing for the boys was the car stereo and it was a race to get as many speakers into the car interior as possible. A kid my age had the most. Twenty-seven. Six in the driver's door, six in the passenger door, four in the back doors, two each under the driver and passenger dash, five along the parcel shelf and two bass boxes in the boot. It was a Nissan Sunny but it drove like a nightclub. The kid had lost his licence to drinking and driving and on Saturday night he just got in the car and listened to the radio with the lights on until the battery went flat then the next day all the boys got together to recharge the kid's car for the next week. It was what the boys did, like leaving the cave for food and fire in the stone-age days. The cars had to be kept charged. I'd have had a car myself but I had other things to do on a Sunday morning and that involved the topless birds in the shiny boots.

When I Was A Kid

When I was a kid I went to the primary school at the end of the road. I didn't bother with learning. I learnt one thing early and that was if you were clever enough you could always get what you wanted without paying. I was a charmer. Little Lee Trebilcock. I went visiting the old dears in the old folks home so they could give me money to buy cigarettes and male contraception. I knew what male contraception was for. It was johnnies to keep the birds quiet. I said it was for my dad in the shop then I blew them up in the park or got my hands wet with the liquid in them. I nicked stuff from Woolworth's on Saturday morning when all the kids were in with their old ones. I nicked small electrical appliances and gave them to my Uncle Septor and he gave me pound coins.

My family name was Trebilcock but we pronounced it Tre-Bill-Coe because my old dear didn't want people thinking we were mutants down our cul-de-sac. It was a Chivermouth name. Some of the kids called me Treble Cocks but I didn't mind. It was all good advertising for me. My old dear got called to the school one time when I was chasing the girls round the playground shouting it out and they'd got scared. It was kiss chase but the girls were frightened it would be more. The kids stopped calling me Treble Cocks after they saw the success I was having.

When I was a kid I didn't attend school regularly in case of missing out. When the teachers started asking questions Uncle Septor wrote in on the backs of brown envelopes. 'This boy's mother is incapacitated by early onset baskets' he told the teachers and he put 'RECYCLED' on the envelope top. I stayed at home and watched the news programmes on the TV, lying on the settee on my special comforter cushion, waiting for the community nurse to come over in her stiff outfit so you could see the line of the knickers through. Or I went into the park and hung around smoking, kicking dry dogs' crap along, drinking Chubby's cola, reading yesterday's wet paper off the shrubbery. Sometimes I rode around in the banana boxes on the back of Uncle Septor's tricycle, stopping off at The King's Limb for half a pint of ale and a cheese sandwich, delivering mail-order pornography and cleaning up the professional girls in Unity Street where Uncle Septor went in alone and came out doing his trousers up.

In the second year of big school I got frightened I was a homosexual when I sat behind Clinton Cord in constructive woodwork. Clinton Cord was a stringy boy in the athletics running team and his trousers always pulled down off his back on the plastic chair so that through the orange bobbly slot you could see the crack of his arse appearing. I got a little boner when I saw that crack. I was making a postcard of Chivermouth money box where the shopping centre picture got stuck on the plywood and Clinton was making a letter tidy. The other kids were on hat racks. I beat Clinton Cord up after boys' domestic science when his was the only soufflé to rise and I ate my chocolate in the yard before.

I was mates with Hawley Harvey Crippon. He went pack-a-sacking round Europe and returned with his virginity lost. I met him afterwards down at the open-air pool and he took his trunks off and put them on his head at the fountain and stood like one of the Italian statues. He said it had been sex with a woman but later he told me it was a man. I gagged and put my cigarette out. He cried. I didn't want Hawley around me with his fucking disease but Hawley was the only one that was nice to me and Hawley grew on you. He was such a little wanker you got absorbed into it.

Hawley worked with antiques in an arcade on the Barbican. He sold pewter condiments and cast-iron ware. It was all old stuff. He couldn't bear anything new around him except for his Posturepedic bed. I didn't mind it when Hawley minced like a girl and there was no-one there except me. He kept paper bags on the corridor steps outside the shop so he had to mince to get them while you got your change out. His family name was Crippon. It was unfortunate that his mother called him Hawley Harvey because it worked out almost the same name as Hawley Harvey Crippen, the doctor that killed his wife and chopped her up in the cellar, but that was just Hawley's mother.

Hawley lived on the housing estate round from ours. Hawley's mother got a housing association house after

Hawley's dad beat her up so much she got a permanently blue cheek and open veins on one side of her face. Hawley's dad was angry at Hawley for being queer and as Hawley's older brother Elwood had gone from Borstal training to three years for breaking and entering, Hawley was all his old man saw of his sons. I knew which pub Hawley's father drank in and I knew the things he said about Hawley when he was drunk but I think he did love Hawley because when Hawley's front teeth got knocked out when he was freewheeling on stabilizers down their road, his old man ran out of the house swearing in his vest and slapped Hawley so hard he nearly cried.

Hawley wore make-up every day of his life, mostly honey complexion foundation and mascara. He said it made him feel better about himself and he had very bad acne as a kid so his face was pitted and it was true. He got beaten up for it because that's what people did in Chivermouth when they saw something different because it scared them or made them want to break out and express and they didn't know how.

Hawley was a needy boy. He got low being the only real homosexual we knew in Chivermouth. There was one queer nightspot, the Club Climax, under the seafront, but it was usually half-full of old men in sailor suits and you got touched up on the dick on the way out through the tunnel. That's if you got past the blokes giving oral serenade against the zigzag rails. I went along with Hawley once a month. He usually got a seafront mouthjob off a slackjaw with a family of grand-children at home. My looks helped him. I never overdrank so I had to use the Gents, if you follow.

It was like the boys' school. The boys' school was for the sons of doctors and lawyers and people we never saw unless we were arrested or ill. It was near our park. I never saw inside. I never knew what went on but it looked like the kids were going for a day's work instead of going to school. They wore little grey shorts suits with long grey and black socks and black sandals. They carried satchels and wore grey caps. They stood around under the arch of their gate and talked to each other. They didn't smoke or lunge around or swear or stand stationary on their bicycles to show off. They didn't have bicycles. They had cycles, expensive mountain bikes for Everest. They didn't chew gum or carry cheap personal stereos that everybody could hear, they just stood and talked. Maybe they even chatted. Or they picked their nails and stroked their chins. Or at least it looked like they did. They looked like the politicians on the telly. They were miniature politicians.

I got into fights with the kids from the boys' school, especially when I knew they got detained for not wearing their hats outside school. I beat up a few and held them under their own forecourt fountain and spat on their fringes and rubbed it in. I wasn't brutal. I tried jamming one runt's ball in his fly and got detained myself. In fact I got a letter home and threatened police action but the old dear was undergoing the baskets just at that time and the teachers felt sorry for me and they could see the kind of stress I was under.

It wasn't like I got away because when I went to work at the Do It Easy I rode regularly past the restrainer walls. The vibration of the heavy bus engine and the fumes through the fire door were nice and relaxing. When the lights went red I could look down into the play lawn and see the kids in glasses posturing and re-enacting Robin Hood around the monkey puzzle trees and I'd get the beginnings of a hefty boner and I'd reposition the peanut butter sandwiches over my lap but it was getting on my fucking nerves.

My Uncle Septor

My Uncle Septor was always barking on about darkies and wogs when they came on the telly or he would say that some people were born better than others and you knew he didn't mean better than him. He ran an exchange and mart business on the estate for all the families that didn't have enough for luxury items. Most families on the estate were members and it meant you could trade in whatever thing you were bored of at the time for whatever your neighbour was bored of. The way it worked was that things like electrical goods, furniture and pets circulated the estate. Our two-piece suite had come from Richard and Majollica and in exchange they got the Alsatian bitch we got from four doors down. We'd gone part-exchange on a boxer puppy and midi hi-fi but the Alsatian wouldn't settle and we passed it on. We'd had beds and got rid of all my kid's stuff. We'd got trainer porn videos with young girls in Swedish accents playing with dolls until their stepfathers appeared and used the dolls to show how to give oral sex to a grown-up man. They used real kids. I grew up on them but we passed them on. I tried them on Hawley but he was always too busy dressing the front window with knick-knacks that turned up from Uncle Septor's garage lock-up − china carthorses with gold-coloured harnesses, spider plants, fun fur puppies curled up in little wicker baskets.

Uncle Septor had been in the electrical trade before he started up the business and he worked the exchanges by word of mouth all over the estate, repairing faults and taking a small cut. He was on the sick and did the exchanging on the side. Sometimes he slipped in a couple of fire-damaged stock items or a good-label video player he'd picked up in the dark from the front room of one of the better houses. He taught

Hawley's brother Elwood everything he knew and Elwood was inside doing a three-year stretch. Hawley said Uncle Septor should find him a man and he probably could. Uncle Septor would have bent over himself if there was a quid in it for him.

Uncle Septor lived at the beginning of our road. His front door was under a redbrick tunnel. All the houses at the beginning of the road had redbrick tunnels. Two houses shared each tunnel and you turned left or right depending on who you wanted. Uncle Septor said the council architects wanted to design something special so the tenants would look after the place but the redbricks got dirty and the kids left plastic tractors, three-wheeler motorbikes and buggies all over the paths and pavements and the older kids drew on the bricks or sprayed them with teenage semen and glue. Uncle Septor said the council should have given them a swimming pool and a bar and that they'd have looked after them better than redbrick tunnels.

That was the way of my road – cats with gummed-up green eyes, nappies prodded to holes with bamboo canes, the wrappers off the girls' panty pads down the white lines. It was worse at the top of the road. Once you got down to mine it was quite luxurious and then you were into the park and you got the flowers, bushes and the rest.

Uncle Septor ran the photography club for the young men of Chivermouth. It was an organisation for single young men to come along and express. He took me through the steps of it when I got on his lap instead of my old man's. They met once a week for slide shows and home videos. They had talks from specialist historians and the youngster members shaved their heads to a quarter of an inch and bought British bulldogs from the dog rescue centre when they had any. I saw the kids around town in small gangs or on the football terraces. It was for artistic expression and it stopped the fights.

Uncle Septor wore Brylon trousers that flared at the knee and wrinkled over the waist. He wore a cardigan and black slip-on boots. He wore a black leather donkey jacket that made him look taller. He was a tall, thin man with eyes like hollow tubes. He had to be quick. He had to keep his eye on the game. He always smelt of smoke. He was away at sea in the merchant navy before I was born. He got a discharge for persistent throat infection. No-one knew what that meant except that the whole of his back was an oriental sea warrior tattoo that moved when he circled his shoulder blades. He was a painted man under the cardigan. He had a panther on his forearm and names and roses. He had BRENDA on his trunks line. He had kids of his own, we just didn't know where or who they were.

For the weekends and the countryside Uncle Septor rode about on a large customized tricycle he'd had designed for him around an auto salvage Robin Reliant. In the rain he wrapped the tricycle in thick blue sheeting and parked it on the front lawn outside his house where he'd knocked the wall down. On the back he'd screwed a laminated sign that said 'End Of Part One' which he got made up by the television station from the late-night advertising breaks. It was written white on black like the words in a Charlie Chaplin movie. Uncle Septor said the birds liked to know there was more coming.

Uncle Septor's trike had low-slung handlebars straddling a big front bouncy wheel and a bench seat for three with him in the middle. Behind there was a ledge of wooden reinforced banana boxes for standing or storing bits and pieces, the axe, baseball bat and so forth. It was as wide as a narrow car and weighty with heavy, overblown beach buggy tyres. It had taken him a long time to get all the bits together for his trike. When he went out on it he wore a black 1970s child chimney sweep leather cap stitched out of chamois triangles and bifocal glasses which looked like goggles. He wore the black leather three-quarter-length coat and black slip-on leather boots. He took the trike to all the classic car shows and won first prize in the interloper section of the Volkswagen Beetle weekend car rally where Volkswagen Beetles toured the country waving at each other until they got to the seaside where they parked, lifted the bonnets, put them down and drove round town being judged up and down the seafront until it was time to go home.

For the Chivermouth Mayor's Parade Uncle Septor dressed up in his Nazi junior rank Waffen SS uniform that he got mail order from Berlin when the wall came down and he rode into town with two mates standing on the back in green coats making Sieg Heil with their arms. He got sandwiched between the jungle-theme Weight Watchers float and the kiddies dressed up as ants and bees on the Open Wildlife Club pick-up. There were skirmishes around the bus station before the parade moved off and Uncle Septor was asked to go home after fighting broke out.

3. Hawley at the Club Climax

Diane painted big fat women lying nude on chaises-longues or serving tennis balls in white kilts or twisting in disco clothing. Sometimes the fat women were dressed in underwear with cocktail glasses. She was known on the Barbican for her keyrings and she'd had a calendar of her women on sale all over Chivermouth one Christmas. She was a nicely put-together, professional type of older bird, one to wear trouser suits, highlight her hair and drive a low car with a black sunroof. Her skin was well-looked after but her eyes were thin and long. She had snake eyes and she knew that the Chivermouth tourists bought anything in the heat of the holiday moment. The fat women didn't buy me. I knew Diane asked Hawley about me when I came and went but I always avoided her. The fat nude birds in the window upset me. It wasn't art. It was life. Diane didn't believe in her fat women. She knew they sold like ice creams sold. You had to buy one or else you didn't feel like you'd been there.

I slipped off the street under a mural of nude men and women joined at the orifice and went along the narrow corridor to the Barbican Precious Items arcade. I passed crouching by Diane's stable door.

—Is that you, Lee Treble Cock? she sung out over the closed slats.

—No, I said and went on.

—Why don't you come in here and show me how you got that name?

Diane was a powerful woman. She had an interest in a modelling school that was run below the aquarium for the older model that could still cut it on the catwalk and her husband Derek was a leading Labour councillor with previous barrister training.

—No thanks.

—Oh, go on. I'm always hearing your name. I could be so good for you.

She was a cat with a dead mouse around a lad and it went against the grain.

—Can't.

—What did you say?

—CAN'T.

—I thought you were calling me names.

—No.

She was a haute couture scud missile brushed all over with Chanel perfume.

—You can call me names if you like.

She laughed.

I wriggled along the wall and stood up at Hawley's stable door. Hawley was bent over with his flat arse high in the air, arranging silverware on the floor.

—Nice arse, I said and Hawley popped his head around.

—Oh, Lee, I thought you were a customer then, he said and winked.

—How's business? I panted.

—Oh, slow. I sold on a nice moleskin sailor boy blazer this morning. Left-hand hang on the trousers.

—How's the old dear?

—Oh, the same. You know, bonkers.

We both knew. Elsa Crippon was getting garden centre pillars for their hallway.

—That's a shame.

—Yeah.

—Old man still getting punchy?

Hawley leant his arm along an HMV stereogram.

—Oh, he's always beating her up but it's not just that, Lee. He found my Michelangelo library book in the bathroom, behind the plasterboard. I'd cut the penises out and stuck them on the insides of my drawers. He opened it at David and knew it was missing something. It's bad enough not being able to wear tights in the house or have house plants but if I play my Margaret Lockwood videos he just smashes up whatever's nearest. Like, you know, my old dear.

Hawley looked up to me. I felt bad at not seeing him more often and for being so tied up with Lorraine and the Do It Easy.

—He's unwound *The Wicked Lady* and had my *South Pacific* on the bathroom cabinet for weeks. He knows I can't reach it down myself.

—Huh.

—Yes, but tonight I'm going to meet my man, Lee. I can feel it. Tonight's the night.

Hawley said every night was the night.

—Could be, I said and kept quiet about menstruating Lorraine.

We went out from Hawley's little shop and across the road into The Good Distiller, a gin house converted to a bar. In the daytime you could go on a tour to see all the old workings if you were a tourist or a French student with a little rucksack on your back. In the evening you could get a lager top before eight or half past when it filled up.

The Chivermouth Barbican was set right on the sea where the river Chiver drained into the Atlantic. Boats and yachts came into the harbour and in history the Chivermouth forefathers shipped to America before the fishing stopped. The Barbican was cobbles and hot dog stands and jewellery shops in a one-way street leading to the marine aquarium and the naval fort. The yachts jumped up and down in the tide and the swans fought each other's necks for slices of bread around benches with diamond-design wire slats for seats. There were bars for drinking, chandlers for sails and fishing bait, oil shops for aromatherapy, frontless gift shops for fun fur seals and dinosaurs, art arcades for antiques, and a famous Polish artist who painted nude men and women on the wall faces while no-one was looking.

Hawley ordered his favourite Brandy Alexander and I had a lager top which was a lad's drink. I paid and we took a shiny, pale table in a corner among plastic cheese plants. We sat down on high-backed chairs with scarlet upholstery pads. I pulled a large glass ashtray towards me and lit up a Fabulously Regal, wetting and dragging the end of the cigarette up into my mouth. I opened my legs up nice and wide for comfort in daywear jeans and lifted the table with both hands, pulling it to rest slightly away from my groin. There were birds by the fruit machine. I sucked the cigarette smoke around my palate and huffed down into my lungs to feel the first hit that came when I only smoked pre-rolled fags on Friday night. I leant back and swallowed a quarter of a pint.

Usually on a night like this I would be at home with the stereo on, flicking through the tapes I'd made of the local radio station continuous music programmes that played late at night and which I timed and recorded. Or I'd be ironing my jeans and rubbing aftershave into the collar of my denim or corduroy shirt depending on the time of year. Later I'd step about in clean pants over car magazines and peanut butter finger rolls trying to get to the mirror to squeeze my nose and sideboard pores which I knew you couldn't see in the dark but which I knew were there.

The Good Distiller was filling up and Hawley got up to use the Gents and fix his face.

When Hawley was seven or eight, before I knew him, he lived in one of the richer parts of Chivermouth. His mother Elsa Crippon was a dental nurse and his father Eric Crippon was a foreman in the American chewing gum factory. Hawley always had lovely teeth. Eric Crippon was always fighting for better hours and better pay in the factory. He was a union man but the unions disappeared or went out and Hawley's father got redundancy when they cut out some of the flavours – rhubarb, star fruit. When Hawley's dad started being at home in the afternoons, he began to notice odd behaviour in Hawley. While Elwood was dressing up with sabres and using under 10s police truncheon sets, Hawley was in his plastic pants and old dear's bedspread singing Bali Ha'i round the lounge which upset his dad seeing as he'd given the best years of his life for the little bleeders. So Eric Crippon started locking Hawley out of the back door when he got dressed up or cried or showed any feminine behaviour. It could have been that Hawley was just taking the female part in his and

Elwood's games. Elwood was a little criminal, but Hawley's dad didn't see it that way and Hawley was stubborn.

Hawley met me on the way home from school after he moved into the housing association house when it was just Hawley, Elwood and Elsa. I'd seen this short, wet-lipped kid in registration and I knew he was beaten up regularly by some of the kids. I needed a light for a fag and I thought I'd ask him for a laugh and then punch the little poof's lights in. Anyway he surprised me by taking out a long thin silver pump-action lighter he'd shoplifted. He gave me a mauve-coloured cocktail cigarette to smoke and said the birds liked them, only he said 'girls' of course, that was Hawley. It turned out I liked the kid. I spent two quid on coloured Russian cocktail fags and the birds did like them. The year after, Uncle Septor got his hands on Elwood, and Hawley and I went to Torquay on the Beaver Line hopper.

I got into some eye contact with one of the birds at the fruit machine. The bird was on heels that pushed her calves right out and she wasn't wearing tights. She had on a tight denim mini skirt and a black polo-neck top that was sleeveless and skintight on her. Her chest was a couple of water balloons. Like the families on my estate who saw what they couldn't have in the magazine adverts and on the satellite telly, this bird was one of the ones that saw fashion fitting everyone, like she could wear any piece of it just because. Her arms were fat in the top and the denim skirt rode her belly into different thicknesses. She'd dyed her thick hair at the roots to stay blonde and her make-up was heavy and black. She could have been one of the Unity Street professional girls. She was drinking orange squash with colourless liquor and she was older than me. I gave her some eye and groin contact where I winked and pushed my groin into the air two or three times like a dog round a bitch. The dog was a bitch and she pressed her knees together pushing the calves out even further like she was double-jointed. She took out a packet of fags from her gold handbag and I lifted my lighter off the table. She came over and leant towards me.

—Got a light? asked the bird as if she wasn't reading my mind.

—I've got a flame, I said, pushing the gas lighter under the tip of her white fag. She sucked hard and looked at me. Her eyelashes were thick and blue like reeds around a pool.

—I needed that. Been giving up.

—Yeah? That's bad for you.

—What, giving up?

—Yeah.

—You're a tease. Where are you from, then?

—Surrey Housing.

—Should've known. You're all sex-mad over there.

—How d'you work that one out?

—Just know. Where d'you work then?

—Do It Easy. Shelving. That's where you'll find me.

—I'll remember that.

—What's your name?

—Theresa. What's yours?

—Lee Trebilcock.

—See you round then, Lee Treble Cock.

The bird laughed and went back to her mate by the fruit machine wall sockets. Hawley came out of the toilet. He'd changed into a flimsy, black see-through rockstar overshirt and his hairless chest was naked underneath. He wore the shirt unbuttoned at the neck and let it hang loose over his stiff pale blue jeans. He wore American high-top trainers only he didn't do the laces up, he just slapped across in them with the jeans tucked into the boots at the ankle. I ran my right hand over my dick and went to the bar. I bought Hawley a double.

Downstairs in the Flaggoners Bar there was a stag night going on with students from the university that used to be a polytechnic. We'd had a student when our house had got on a tenancy resident list by mistake. A youth enrolled on to a marine biology course had turned up in a fleecy purple jacket and pair of tan hiking boots saying that he was quiet and he'd do the washing-up. I'd got rid of him but I didn't like students. Now one of the stags had got his dick out into his pint and was swilling up froth and there was a half-dressed policewoman stripper over a bar stool with baby lotion covering her arse which wasn't a bad arse. I looked away and Theresa from the fruit machines came back over on her heels.
—Lee Treble Cock.

I felt raw with the dick's dick in his pint and Hawley feeling so low.
—Yeah.
—Where you off to tonight?
—Club Climax.
—What – you're not—
—Yeah. I'm a poof.
—Oh. I see. You cheeky cunt.
—Sorry, love. Born that way. See you round, Theresa.

I went back to Hawley and watched him caress his thin finger through his fringe. What was there for Hawley in Chivermouth?
—Nothing, Hawley said absentmindedly, happy now that the Brandy Alexanders were relaxing him.

We left The Good Distiller and idled across the one-way main street of the Barbican. Hawley stopped to look in at a row of brass boilers and kettles strung on to the window bar of an antique junk shop. I called in to Captain Ahab's Cod

House and bought a cardboard cup of chips. We wandered along by the sea where the tide was up by the harbour and where the boats and yachts hung around magically moored. They swung and creaked a little. We ran our fingers over the tops of the granite bollards. Hawley said he'd like to find a man that size, the size of a granite Barbican bollard. I had an inexplicable boner.

We walked on to the cobbles and up the low slope that takes you off the Barbican and on to the front in the shadow of the hotels and the fortress buildings with the marine-life aquarium. We walked up into the remembrance statues with the lists of soldiers that died in the war and the historical wayfaring discoverers that sailed off from Chivermouth in the sixteenth century. I didn't know all the history but I knew the feel and it was calm and nice for Hawley who liked statues. We walked down from the grass past the yacht club and down the five or six zigzag stepcases tacking down the hill to the sea. We went under the tunnel and passed a bouncer in fingerless gloves. It was early. The queers were still asleep in their coffins.

When we got down to the stable door of the Club Climax, a blonde bird was sitting on a stool with her skirt ridden right up her thighs but she had hairy calves and you could see that she wasn't a bird at all. Hawley paid for two passes and we got ultraviolet stamps on our hands so you could pass in and out for oral shagging and what not. The transvestite swung the stable door open and we shimmied past. Once inside, we stepped along a dark, bouncy green-carpet landing, the type of landing you got in a walk-in house of horror at the fairground but instead of skeletons and ghosts there were big pictures of Marilyn Monroe with teeth like mortuary slabs. We passed black and white prints of Audrey Hepburn in *Roman Holiday* and Hayley Mills in *The Moon-Spinners*.

Further along there was a full-length of John Wayne with a gun holster. Hawley knew the way. He often came on his own. Ha ha. I didn't get my own joke, I thought as I followed his translucent shirt down the corridor.

At the end of the landing you went two ways – downstairs to the main bar and dance floor or up spiral steps to the snug and observation balcony. Hawley made for the staircase down and I went with him, stepping on the neon-lit carpet steps that were just too wide so you had to lunge. The bar was at the end of the room so you had to cross the dance floor to get to it. Hawley swung his arm easily around a dancing podium. Once at the bar, he got up on a stool and took out a ten pound note which he waved. A large Latin-origin barman put down a thick book and came over from his stool. Hawley ordered a Señorita Loves Curaçao cocktail which arrived in a man-shaped glass with a couple of cherries and a mini gherkin. I took a bottle of Canadian beer and joined Hawley on a stool. The DJ, in a glass pod overlooking the floor, was playing a twelve-inch remix of an Irish stadium band number-one chart hit. It had a driving beat with a bird wailing over the top of it like a cat had got up into her knickers. Hawley shook his shoulders and threw his head back.

Hawley wasn't a bad-looking bloke although it was clear to see why the birds had stayed away. He had an open face with blue eyes and short blond hair that he tried to wear clumped into little cherubic angel curls. He always used foundation make-up so when he sweated it ran off his face in a slide. His eyes always looked theatrical because of the eye-liner and mascara he wore and he looked like he was a guest on a television show where the make-up artist had gone too far to brighten him for the studio lights. He had a thick neck and wide waist with a flat arse and little rugby player's legs.

The DJ acknowledged us from his pod and played at majorettes with his next twelve-inch record, swirling it in the air by the little hole in the middle of the vinyl. He pulled the stylus across his turntable and wrestled off the headphones with one hand. He opened the top of the pod as if it was a racing car and climbed out on to his ladder. He got down and came over.

—Hawley!

Brian and Hawley had been lovers briefly up against one of the zigzag railings for half an hour one night.

—Brian.

—Haven't seen you for a while. Not since the last time.

Brian had a collection of art deco tea sets which Hawley'd had a mind to getting his hands on until it turned out Brian was a desperate, violent man with a wife, two kids and a French poodle.

—Been busy, Bri. This is my friend, Lee Trebilcock.

—Trebilcock, eh?

—That's me, I said. One for the birds.

—Ooh, seen you before, you're a challenge, said Brian as he turned on his heel. Got a mate from the music industry coming down tonight, Hawley, he called over his shoulder as he walked back to his ladder. Doing a review for a national club mag. He's just right for you.

Back in his pod, Brian put on a leather cowboy hat and pretended to do redneck country dancing. Hawley started jigging about on his stool and the club was filling up. There were several older men in suits at the bar, leaning on their elbows with their arses shoved out at right angles. Some of them played nurse to cocktails and other sipped on long tube glasses of Canadian beer. On the floor, a boy in green fluorescent cycling shorts was cirling his hips to the music. In one of the circular booths, a couple of boys were rubbing each other and biting each other's neck. A girl and a boy sat talking next to them. An old woman with a bottle of Guinness and a special glass sat by them. The boy on the dance floor got up on to a podium and began to gyrate his hips, doing the actions of bread-making with his hands. I could do that dancing but I wasn't doing it here. A drunk man in a grey suit went to the dance floor and jiggled about like a Bee Gee. He took off his tie and undid his shirt top button. We looked on and more blokes came down the stairs and over the floor under the mirror balls.

A bloke in a fleecy lumberjack shirt came over and blew on my neck. I turned round and hit him. He went down and was pulled back up by his boyfriend, a girl in a hooped Scarlett O'Hara afternoon dress. Hawley stroked my arm and the lumberjack spat. The barman came over and lifted up the lid of his bar entrance. He came round and told me to calm down or get out. I said I was calm. The barman said he didn't want trouble. I finished my bottle and ordered another.

I took the cap off a beer bottle with my teeth and a man came over. The man started talking to Hawley, leaning on Hawley's knees. The man was straight-looking. He was wearing snow-washed denims the Rastafarians had made popular eight or so years before. He had plain, dark hair and a face I'd already forgotten. I caught it with mine in the wall mirrors. It had white skin and heavy eyebrows. The man was older than us, perhaps thirty-three or four. His hair was grey in places and his eyes too. He looked like he thought a lot because his brow hung over the top of his face. He looked like he'd made himself. He looked like he had a secret. On top he wore a cream cotton jumper from one of the high street family stores.

I had brown curly sideboards of facial hair, brown eyes, thin lips and a gap between my front teeth which could have worked against me but didn't. I had quick eyes that swivelled easily so I was always abreast of the game.

Hawley chattered on and then I felt him tugging at the sleeve of my leather jacket.

—Lee, this is Alun Glenhusky. He's down from London. He's doing a review of the Club Climax. He knows Brian.

—Oh yeah, I shouted back, unimpressed.

—Hi, Lee. Pleased to meet you, said Alun Glenhusky and the evening became night.

Alun took us over to one of the circular nesting booths and swept the dirt off the vinyl with the palm of his hand. He sat us down and went to the bar, returning with a tray of bright green Signor Dabbles in Menthe cocktails. Hawley and I took the glasses down and put them on the table and Alun swished off back to the bar holding the tray between both hands. When he came back he asked us what we both did. Hawley said he had an antique shop on the Barbican.

—Just small, Hawley fluttered. Condiments and that sort of thing. Silverware, glass. Cast-iron pots. I love to use cast-iron. I take them home sometimes and bring them back in the morning all washed up, he blushed. Lee works in the Do It Easy, don't you, Lee?

—Yeah.

—And does he? Alun asked Hawley, winking.

—Does he what?

—Do it easy?

—Ha ha, Alun. Lee's a tom-cat with the birds, aren't you, Lee?

I could see Hawley liked the bloke and I wished him luck.

—Yeah, I returned. I turned my back to them slightly to let them get on with it. They were getting on well. Brian must have sent him over. I looked up to the pod and saw Brian in silhouette tipping the brim of his cowboy hat to a dance-floor kid in faded jeans and black hobnail boots. The kid had the short sleeves of his black T-shirt rolled up to his armpits and he was jigging up and down on the spot a couple of feet from the bar. Eventually Brian got down out of his pod and took the kid up the stairs.

—What do you think of the Club Climax then, Lee? asked Alun.

—S'all right. Not really my cup of tea. I'm not queer.

—Nor am I. Well, I am, but I'm straight too.

—What – you mean you go in for the birds?

—Yes.

Hawley looked like the cat that got the clotted cream.

—Greedy one, are you?

—No. Not really.

—What – they're all at it in London, are they?

—They're undecided. There's freedom of choice, you know.

—Yeah, I know, I said and looked at Hawley. I turned away again and watched the dancers circling each other, offering up their groins for inspection.

—I'm going upstairs, I said and left.

Upstairs the music wasn't so loud and it was darker. I passed a couple snogging on the stairs, lit from the back by a Climax neon flashing nameplate. It looked like they were getting there. Further up it looked like a bloke was pissing into another's mouth but it was just oral sex. I climbed through the pleasure carcasses and headed for the small bar on the observation balcony. From there I could see Hawley and Alun Glenhusky moving in for a snog. Hawley was wriggling his legs in the seat like a kid with ice cream before the main cinema programme. He looked innocent in that place. He put his lips forward and held them against Alun's without moving them or opening his mouth. I knew this was the screen-star kiss he talked about. They stuck there for minutes and Alun didn't try to get his tongue in. Hawley had his eyes closed. Alun was looking down and concentrating. His hand moved on to Hawley's thigh and began to massage it. Hawley squirmed and moved closer, reaching happily for Alun's groin. I looked away and felt something start in my eye like a small drop of water or something. I wiped at it and ordered another bottle. I stood around with my hands in my jeans pockets, trying to hide my packet. I felt old man looks on me as I put my head back and swallowed the beer. I heard 'nice' as I lit a Fabulously Regal, running the lighter down my jeans to get a flame. The music had changed. Brian had slowed it down. I recognised Diana Ross singing 'Upside Down' from the 1980s. That was the trouble with the Climax. It always climaxed with grandaddy music. The kid in the black T-shirt came up the stairs coughing and choking. He'd come in from outside. The queer that came in from the cold. He had a film of sperm around his face. Nobody noticed. His shirt bib was wet. He was followed by Brian.

—Hey, Mr Treble Cock! Don't shout that name in here. You'll have them all after you.

I ignored him.

—Your mate's doing well with Alun Glenhusky.

I dropped my beer bottle on the edge of the counter and walked back down taking the stairs two at a time.

Hawley was exchanging telephone numbers with Alun. He saw me and ran over.

—Ready to go now, Lee.

—Come on then.

Outside, the fresh air hit Hawley like a smack on the forehead. He got his breath back and his eyes jumped. I closed my jacket against the one a.m. cold and the seafront cowboys playing Christ's last stand in the crucifix offer position.

We went back to Captain Ahab's and ordered a couple of six-inch ham and pineapple pizzas. We might usually have gone for one twelve-inch but Hawley wanted a six-inch all to himself. We took the pizzas back down to the sea and to the small concrete beach that was covered with waves.

In the shelter on the tiny cliffside a tramp was sleeping it off. The sea was wild and it crashed up on to the walkway and zigzag railing making us wet. Hawley woke the tramp and moved him on. He was giggling and he took off his socks and shoes and stood right in the tops of the waves as they broke on to the Greek temple steps. I stood with him. The tramp stood and ate our pizzas. Hawley screamed and I shouted 'fuck you, fucking cunt' and our clothes stuck to us.

Hawley's rockstar shirt stuck on to his chest and his hair frothed with the moulding treatments he used. His honey foundation slipped down off his skin and got washed away and I saw his face. His eyes blackened like bruises as he rubbed the sockets with his knuckles. The sea was so loud I couldn't hear or see. I was drunk. I was angry. I didn't know.

I wanted to turn and kiss Hawley hard on the lips and use my tongue to open up his mouth and carry on kissing him until the waves pushed us on to our knees and I could unzip his clinging, stiff jeans and pull down his pants. I felt something in my eye that was more than salt water.

When we got back, there was a note from my old dear asking me to let the cat out but we'd never had a cat and I put the video on and played *Power Machines Big Truck Racing* until I saw Hawley start to cry. I pretended to ignore him as I reached through the serving hatch for a can of lager but I heard him.

Hawley had curled himself up on the settee and was crying into my TV pillow. His feet were nudging at the china window sill carthorses. He was dribbling into the settee cover and clenching his fists. I sat down beside him and put my arm on his back. His body was warm and he didn't move, he just carried on crying. I moved my arm and squeezed him with my hand. His back was bony and going up and down with crying. It didn't stop. I reached into the warm place where his face and tears were and I put my fingers under his wet chin. I lifted his face out of the pillow and looked into his eyes.

—I feel happy, Lee, Hawley said, blowing a saliva balloon out of his mouth.

His eyes cried for me to stop the tears and I reached and put my other arm around his back. I put my face close to his and breathed on it like it was an animal that had recently died. He laughed.

I nuzzled him and laughed and kissed him on the side of the head. He moved his face around and held it up. I looked at his lips and closed my eyes and kissed his mouth. He opened his mouth and wound his fingers around my leather jacket. I kicked over the beer can and we both lay along the settee. I held him to me while he cried into my chest and undid my shirt and kissed it all off. He undid his jeans and put his hand in. He took my hand and put it in too. He moved his hand over my hand. Then he moved his body backwards and forwards and unzipped my jeans. He put his other hand on my dick. Our dicks were like little flowers in our hands. We touched them and held them and we touched and held each other.

The next morning I awoke to find Hawley with his hand in my pants and his head on my knee and I told the dirty pervert to get the fuck out of it.

4. The Student with the Twat's Haircut

On Sunday mornings I liked to lie awake with a bit of manual stimulation and Karen Carpenter on the bedside Awakener. I'd climax to 'Please Mr Postman' and it was a nice cosy scene of romantic self-abuse. I used Uncle Septor's banned Scandinavian literature he got on a drinkathon to Stockholm. I liked to have a few words and a couple of pictures. You couldn't get ejaculating dicks in England and the Scandinavian birds were spicy and continental with big blue eyes and blonde hair. The magazines were small and handy to hold and they used different locations like snowy mountains and farmyard animals on haybeds. At Christmas they used cattle in a little hut with shepherd actors and a virgin actress and not a babe in swaddling-bands in sight. The pictures were always one to a page so that you could follow the story like a book and you didn't know what was coming next and ha! I never did. I always forgot. I had quite a large collection.

My favourite was the man who walks into the backstreet Norrköping bookshop and asks the busty bird assistant to reach down an almighty atlas from up high on a shelf. The bird's in a short mini-kilt and as she goes up the ladder you see she's in completely see-through knickers and sheer suspenders. I've never experienced knickers like it in real life. They were like cling film. There are no words in this story except the odd Scandinavian cunt word and the bird reaches down the book and the two agree by facial expression to leave the shop and go to her house where she's got her randy mate waiting in a bikini on a chaise longue. They get down to it on the patio and it shows the squeezing of the tight see-through knickers and the bloke's face contorting and the bookshop bird's face being covered by the randy mate handling and aiming the translucent liquid that gets in all their eyes.

I used the out-of-date home shopping catalogues and turned to the underwear pages. I liked the little cotton and nylon mounds and as the girl models bent to show off the pattern and line lying neatly across net curtain four-poster beds, I would flit my eyes to the words and read off the sizes and cotton-mix ratios of the panties. Pants were for wearing, knickers for pulling off and panties for sucking on while the bird was squirming into your mouth against the Pay and Display machine. I liked the brunette models. I wasn't a pervert or desperate or anything. I just liked to relax with an inanimate cunt and be reminded of what it was like under the birds' clothes without all the Friday night car park hassle. Usually in real life the knickers were wrinkled and riding up the arse once you got there as they'd been over a disco floor a hundred times or more. I wasn't a romantic twat that reckoned all heaven lived there in that tiny triangle. I understood women. What kind of bird would stand about in her underpants on shiny pages between indoor putting sets and maxi hi-fi if they weren't enjoying it? There was something about turning over to the power drills, too, like you could imagine doing it to a bird with a hammer drill. Working at the Do It Easy had got me into that, admiring the hand-size electric drill bodies and marvelling at the smooth dullness of the largest drill bits which were an inch and a half thick. Thing was, you'd ruin a cunt with a thing like that.

I was reading through a Hot Wives Confession in the back of one of Uncle Septor's 1970s out-of-print manuals when the phone rang. I carried on reading Sue Sealed In Rubber when I heard shouts from the bottom of the stairs.

—Lee! Someone wants you!

It was Majollica, my old dear's mate from over the road. She always put the frozen dinners in the oven on a Sunday in case the old dear was having a turn and couldn't remember what the cooker was for.

—Someone wants you!

Someone, I thought. Make that everyone. I pulled my tired foreskin hard up over my slightly cracked helmet.

—Lee!

I pushed the cover down and wiped my hands with an easy-reach tissue ball. I pulled on pyjama bottoms and walked out on to the landing, padding on the bottoms of the trouser legs.

—Yeah, I said, reaching the phone ledge and grabbing the receiver off Majollica who gave my chest a nice look but Majollica was nearly fifty.

—Is that you, Lee? a bird's voice asked.

—Yeah. Who's this?

—It's Lorraine. I'm at the hospital. Ray's taken a tumble on the dry-ski slope. He's broken his leg. I don't know who else to turn to. His dad's on the rigs.

—Sorry, love. It's Sunday. My day off.

—Lee. It's me. Lorraine.

—No can do. I'm a busy boy at the weekends. How did you get this number?

—Ronald. He's down here, too. I don't know what to do.

—Yeah, look, Lorraine, sorry I can't help.

I put the phone down and it rang again.

—Yeah.

—Lee!

—Clear this line, Lorraine. I'm expecting a call. Bloke's calling about a dog. Get off the line.

I hung up and heard Uncle Septor's voice in the lounge.

—Trouble with the birds, son?

Uncle Septor always called me son.

—No. Just some bird and her boy, that's all.

—Anything I can help you with?

—No.

—Get us an ale then.

I reached around the serving hatch and grabbed a couple of tins.

—Only got lager, I said and we cracked open the thin metal tops, sat down on the settee and started to drink.

—Septor! shrieked the old dear from the kitchen.

—Here, Wendy.

—Septor, that cat's been in here again spraying on the furniture. I can smell him all over that settee.

The old dear poked her head round the serving hatch and got some air. Her hair was coming out her short pony tail and her pink ribbon was trailing on to her shoulder. She was wearing an apron.

—He's been here. I know it. He gets in at night. I can smell him.

We carried on talking.

—How's life then, son?

—All right.

I suddenly thought of the time I stuck a rocket up the arse of the black cat that used to sleep on the slimy front garden gumming up its eyes.

—All right.

—Bit of trouble?

—No.

—Why don't you come along to the club one of these weeks?

—Dunno.

—Might be just your thing. Just right for a young lad wanting to express. We're always needing new blood. Strong, healthy lad like you, he winked, if you're interested I'll get you in. You can come along. You've seen what we do.

—Yeah.

—Wednesday night, then. Seven o'clock at Chubby's for a confidential venue.

—Maybe.

—Saw your young mate last night.

—Which one?

—Hawley Crippon. Getting out of a cab with a man. You want to tell him to watch out. He'll get himself into trouble with that. People in Chivermouth don't like that sort of thing.

—What sort of thing?

—Poofs, lad. Not natural.

—He's no longer my mate.

—What did he do. Try it on?

I stayed silent. I knew one word from me could land Hawley in a hospital bed next to Lorraine's crippled Ray.

—Did he try it on with you, the fucking little poof?

—Yes, I said.

—Fucking little queer. Don't you worry. We'll sort him out.

Uncle Septor was angry. The tattoos on his brown forearms stood out. He flexed the sides of his lager tin with his nicotine fingers and jostled his front denture on to his tongue. His thick black plastic-rimmed glasses toppled down on to his nose. He took up the TV remote control and switched on to the Sunday soap opera omnibus.

—Fucking queers. We'll fix them. Don't you worry, Lee lad, he tapped my knee and finished the can, slapping it down on the poof, we'll get him. Don't you worry.

The old dear shimmied through on shaky pins.

—That you, Frank?

—Frank's gone, barked Septor. Left you years ago. It's Septor, love.

—Oh, I thought it was Frank.

—It's Septor. Sep-tor!

—The old man's gone, I said.

—Someone's got my Frank. I think they've killed him.

—All right, love. Sit down. It's your brother-in-law here now.

—Oh. Peach slice, then, Lee?

I left the house and walked up the cul-de-sac in the direction of Hawley's house.

My old dear had got stuck in a rut when she was thirty-nine and it wasn't just the baskets. She'd gone back to being a kid, putting ribbons in her grey hair and wearing short dresses she took up on the sewing machine. She had the legs of a girl, an old girl. They were unshaped but thin and her hips were wide so a skirt hung off the ledge of them. She wore short skirts or short dresses. Not miniskirts. Just short clothes. And cardigans. She'd got stuck in the 1970s. In the summer Majollica had to go down on to the Barbican and buy flip-flops for her. The old dear's family didn't want her to marry the old man, they said he wasn't good enough for her. She'd already had an offer from her cousin but they didn't know if it was legal and he was forty-eight. The old dear was thirty-two and unmarried and she worked in a baker's piping jam and my old man had wanted her potato and cheese slices at eleven o'clock every morning.

The old dear's face was plain. Her hair was grey through the affliction and her skin was red. She didn't look very old. She just looked like she was in another place most of the time and she was. She thought Uncle Septor was the old man and she didn't know who I was but the doctors told us that's what happens and that she could get incontinent. Majollica looked after her mostly.

Majollica was a redhead on yellow mules from over the road. She came over twice a day in a pink checked slippery overall and dusted round the old dear's dolls with her special hoover nozzles. Majollica nearly got me inside her house when I was school age.

Before Richard retired from the council drains, Majollica used to sit out on a folding chair on her lawn smoking cigarettes and listening to the local radio. She wore a yellow fluffy house robe and had her hair up in a net. By late afternoon she'd got into her slippery overall and brought out a plastic tub of polishes and household sprays. She'd come out with a cordless telephone and Richard would phone her up two or three times to say where he was in his daily job of sanitation and sewage clearance. When Richard phoned Majollica she spoke very loudly so the whole road knew where he was and what she was saying. By five, in summer, she'd have dry-roast nuts and pecans out on the barbecue rack and Richard would get home in his washed down council-issue waterproofs and they would sit down with Cinzanos. Majollica was around fifty and Richard was older at sixty. They had two grown-up kids that came by on the weekend with toddlers each.

By early afternoon I would be on my way home from school and I would see Majollica sitting outside her redbrick home on her uncut grass and she would be looking up and down the road for whoever was passing so she could be the first to know. When she saw me she would shout 'hey, Lee' at me and open her legs in the house robe so I could see she wasn't wearing any old people's knickers. 'Hey, Lee,' Majollica would shout and I would walk right by. One time she shouted 'hey, Lee, your mum's in here,' and I went up her path and on to her grass and I looked down her robe at her withered up old elephant tits. 'Right in here,' she had said looking straight at my crotch. 'Come in and see'.

Hawley wasn't in. His dad said the bloody little bleeder had gone to the matinee performance of the Chivermouth pantomime version of *Little Women* where the traditional women's roles were taken by men including Brian from the Club Climax. I went into Hawley's room and scratched a swastika on his distressed pine chest-of-drawers. His dad patted me on the shoulder.

—Can't you get any sense into the little bleeder?

—Dunno.

—It's a disease with him.

—Yeah, I agreed and Eric went back downstairs to where he and Elsa were relaxing with mail-order nature videos.

When Eric had gone I took out the top drawer of the chest-of-drawers and looked around for the cut-out penises from the Michelangelo book and when I found them I stamped on them. Then I opened up the bottom drawer and pissed on all of Hawley's glossy ladies underwear. There was so much piss it came right through the drawer and all along the carpet to the edge of the door until I stopped it with my foot and stamped it into the thin carpet.

When I got back, the old dear was napping upstairs. Uncle Septor was asleep on the settee and the phone was off the hook. I replaced the receiver and it rang immediately. I half-expected it to be Lorraine but it was Hawley.

—Lee? People who wanted something off you when you'd never really had a dad.

—No.

—It's Hawley Harvey.

—Go away.

—You came and scratched a swastika on my tallboy. My dad told me.

—You're a stinking pervert. You'll get it, poofter.

—I fancy you, Lee, he whined.

—Fuck off.

—I want you to come over for a rub down.

—What about that Alun Glenhusky one?

—He's come down from London. He's going back soon. His girlfriend's pregnant with twins.

I put the phone down. Uncle Septor tried to roll over in his sleep but the settee stopped him. He folded his arms over his cardigan and opened his mouth. He breathed through that while I opened another can. Then he opened his eyes and closed his mouth.

—All right, son?

—Yeah.

—Don't forget Wednesday. Seven o'clock. Chubby's chip shop.

—I won't.

Uncle Septor got the trike out. While he was pulling the blue plastic sheeting off, I got into a cream Sunday evening

EasyMan woolly jumper. Uncle Septor wheeled the trike off the grass on to the road and sat up on the seat, switching on the enging and revving with the handlebar. He reached round and lifted up the lid of the banana boxes, taking out the leather cap and putting it on his head. I came out and over the road and swung up into one of the passenger seats. Uncle Septor reversed into a parking space, pulled around and moved off up the road.

It was a bumpy ride on Uncle Septor's trike and there was only a safety belt for the driver so I held on with my arm lightly running along the back of Uncle Septor. He sat hunched low down on to the Harley Davidson handlebars, flicking his wrist to slow and accelerate and as we stopped at lights, he twisted his head around at the few bits of traffic to check they were looking at him. I looked around too, with my arm casually lying along the back of the seat, and I winked quietly at the birds clicking along in their shoes for their evening behind club bars or on street corners. We drove through the dockyard past the men waiting outside the Brown Bear for opening time and we smelt the smell of salty sea air and vinegar from Captain Ahab's along the drag to the seafront. Uncle Septor concentrated on the road and took the corners neatly on three wheels, lurching off balance and regaining across the white lines. It wasn't cold and the dust from the road got up in my eyes so I clenched them shut and just looked in the direction of the cars and pavements. Uncle Septor was the middle-aged trike hog of Chivermouth and I was willing pillion hogster.

At the bus station he pulled over on to double yellow lines and stopped. I climbed off, shaking my legs down through so I didn't topple around after the velocity and corners. Uncle Septor snapped open the banana boxes and buried the leather travel cap in wooden-handled implements. He put the keys under his cardigan into his shirt breast pocket. We ducked our heads for no reason and pushed our way through the sway door into The King's Limb.

It was only just open at seven o'clock but already the tables were full. In our path was a black and white sheepdog lying up against a stool. Holding it was a bird in mostly her own skin with a home-made sheepskin jerkin stitched around her waist to a top shirt. It looked more like she was just wearing the sheepskin, it wasn't cut into a coat. She had bare arms with a bangle squeezing three-quarters of the way up the flesh and heavy industrial lace-up boots on her feet. She was sitting with a man in green corduroy trousers who was turning his comfortable shoe over on to its side to lean into her face. Uncle Septor said he was a customer when we got to the bar. He ordered two pints of Friar's Water real ale for us. Uncle Septor drank beer and I drank lager but it was Uncle Septor's shout. Some people's regular alehouse is their second home. The King's Limb was Uncle Septor's first home. His house in our road was for sleeping, exchange work, fencing fancy gear and pimping the comprehensive sixth-formers.

The interior of The King's Limb was dominated by the bar. There were cut-out beer barrels for stools and oak trees for table bases. The ceiling was made of low dark beams. The floor was made of slates. There were two entrances and a back exit. The left entrance brought you in past three upmarket tables, a dusty serving hatch and a dull gold-coloured food hotplate. The right side brought you up to the bar past a fag machine and a CD jukebox with all the old hits of Uncle Septor's youth – 'House of the Rising Sun', 'Blueberry Hill' and all the hits of Elvis. Further on through were tables in makeshift booths with wooden dividing struts. The crapper was on the way through the back exit. Soft drugs got exchanged in The King's Limb and the police force waited at the back under the crapper window when it was time for them to get in there after the criminals. And there were criminals. Elwood Crippon might have been alongside me at the Do It Easy if it hadn't been for Uncle Septor and The King's Limb.

Uncle Septor had his portrait above the fireplace in The King's Limb. It was painted by the Barbican artist who specialized in nude body exterior murals and tramp embalming. He knew Septor of old and had already offered free head embalming when the time came but he also wanted to capture Uncle Septor and he'd oiled up a quick canvas interpretation one afternoon, concentrating on his head with the trike fuzzy in the distance like a photograph. The artist had signed it for Uncle Septor. In return Uncle Septor found plump women to model for the artist's religious and classic illustration work he was experimenting with.

Uncle Septor and I took our pints and went through to the back where the old boys drank. Birds' eyes lifted off delicate glasses and travelled along with us as we wiggled past chairbacks and sharp table corners. Most of the drinkers at the front were young, dressed in heavy boots and sticky blond dreadlock hair. The birds were either in tight gear squeezing them in toothpaste tube action or they were belted and wrapped into leathers straight off the animal. Further back the older ones sat at tables using chairbacks to sit up straight like old folk, tins of tobacco open in front of them and grubby half-full pint sleevers unchanged for luck at each refill. They were dipping their fingertips into moist worms of tobacco and packing it into fag papers.

At the furthest table there were more Uncle Septors of different ages, men with greying hair, grey stubbly chins, bifocal glasses, false teeth. Two of them were roaring at each other from separate tables like they were lions. They just kept roaring and the girl with the long sheepskin jerkin walked by with her arm bangle close to my eyes. The jukebox played loudly of a time when a grown-up bloke ate banana fudges all day and dressed into a flared white studded trouser suit to sing in the evening times. And the man called himself Elvis the Pelvis and died on the crapper so he got winched off. 'Love me tender, love me true . . .' I knew the words and what Uncle Septor's eyes would be doing which was getting moist like the tobacco in the tobacco tins.

The men at the furthest table sat around like men positioned for the night round the wood. They couldn't move except to go to the bar or piss through the exit. They could get smoky bacon crisps or a basket of chips off the hot-plate. They rolled cigarettes, drank, smoked, belched, wiped, sat back, sat forward, leaned, swivelled, roared and looked around and waited. To see what would happen that time. I drank quarter of a pint and sat down and waited too.

—Septor. The men nodded and carried on waiting.

—Boys, Uncle Septor answered, nodding as he reached for his tobacco tin. I had fags left from Friday night and I lit up, leaving the packet and lighter on the table next to my pint. Uncle Septor kept drinking at the crooked hat of his toby jug and I looked round the bar.

Sometimes you got a student or two in The King's Limb and over in one corner it looked like there was a couple taking out books and looking at them. They looked like all the rest of the Chivermouth students, like they'd just got off a weekend for two in a dried-up riverbed. They were wearing the fleecy jackets and hiking boots and sweatshirts without logos on the front. There were four of them in this group, two blokes, two birds with pints. I didn't like to see a bird with a pint. No class. Anyway the birds were scrawny ones all wrapped up in turquoise fleece and wind protectors. It was mostly marine biology up at the university and I stayed away. The blokes had girls' hands and they sipped at their half pints. One of them had a rockabilly's quiff hairstyle that curled over his forehead like a tidal wave going back on itself. There was no need for it. 'It's a free world' they would say in their northern fucking accents. There was no need for a free world that gave you twats. Uncle Septor was right. Tolerance gets you nowhere. I wasn't a fighting boy unless someone provoked me and this kid was provoking me. It was a girl's haircut. He was a bloke. The group was waving its arms to speak and one of them knocked their sandwiches to the floor so the sheepdog had to crawl over nervously on its front to eat them. There was no need for that. The bird in the sheepskin jerkin held on to an upstrut and swayed. A young bald man watched from the bar in a grey felt trench coat. The CD jukebox played 'There is a house in New Orleans' through cracked speakers on 1970s wallmounts.

—My nephew Lee, said Uncle Septor.

—Youngster, the men nodded at me. I nodded back.

There were six men around the table. Two were right on the square corners so the points pricked their abdomens. There was one big ashtray in the middle of the table where the clear wrappings of fag packets uncurled from their tight balls. The men looked ready for something and their eyes were sharp from behind their plastic-rimmed glasses. I knew a couple of them and they were single, bachelors or widowers. Some of them had kids. One was big with dark hair down his scalp sides. His eyes were wayward so he saw double and his corrective lenses were thick. He wore a gold ring on one hand but I knew there wasn't a woman walking around Chivermouth with the other half of it on her finger.

—Lee's expressed an interest in the photography club.

The men took draws on their rolled cigarettes and watched the smoke come out of their mouths.

—You want to be a photographer?

The man talking to me was the same age as Uncle Septor and it looked like he'd come up on the same tracks. He was dressed in a shiny thin brown leather sports jacket which I knew had a waist strap around the back because I'd seen the style before. The jacket had thin lapels and sewn-on pockets with hand flaps. The man had the same skin as Uncle Septor, skin that was rigid enough to hold dust, and he had seven o'clock shadow like grey porcupine needle stubs. His teeth were yellow and his eyes discoloured through years of concentrating on joining together fine oblong fag papers and lighting up. His eyes had seen the bars of Chivermouth through the thick distort of a circular piece of beer glass bottom. I knew the man's name. It was Reg. I knew Reg didn't change his glass when it was time for a new pint.

—Slide shows and that.

—First time?

—Yeah.

—Got a subject in mind?

—Not particularly.

—Ever used a camera?

—Yeah. When something's got me going.

—When you've been moved to record a scene?

—Yeah. When I've been moved.

—Think you've got what it takes?

—Yeah. Name the snap.

—Far corner, left-hand side.

—What d'you want? Family portrait?

—Head and shoulders.

—Okey dokey, I said and got up off the small stool that had

been squeezing my arse. I headed for the students in the corner.

—'Scuse me, mate, I said to the student with the twat's haircut. Come outside for a moment?

—What for? said the student.

—Got to talk to you for a sec. Won't take long. It's in your interest.

The student looked at his mates and laughed.

—Well, if you insist, he said. I don't know what you're going to tell me though. He laughed again and the birds laughed too.

—It's worth waiting for, I said and went out through the back-passage exit. The student followed. In the fresh air, the student hung on one leg looking like he didn't understand. It was dark in the passage to the car park. There was a white light in a ridged plastic slimy cover on the wall.

—Is this far enough? he asked. His face was open and friendly like the open and friendly people that tell you your old dear's barking bonkers.

—Yeah. That's far enough.

—Well, what is it that's so secret?

—It's your hair, mate.

—My hair? What is this?

—Your fucking hair. It's fucking annoying.

—Excuse me, please.

—Your hair is a fucking eyesore and I'm the one that's got to sit in the room with you. You're spoiling my pint. Do you get it? Your head's fucking rude.

The student went to the door so I took the hair by my right hand and pulled the head down by it so I could get the power with my left knee to smack the student in the nose. I let him fall back against the wall and then I used my own head to nut him hard on the forehead. He put his hands to his head and

I lifted my left leg and kicked him hard in the groin. He put his knees together and held his groin with both hands, bending over. I swung my left leg into his stomach and kicked him so he fell over and then I kicked his face once and his right kidney twice because the other one was covered by his body. He lay on the floor and tried to curl his groin up to his head. Perhaps he thought he could lick it better.

—It's your fucking hair, you fucking twat, I said and took out a cigarette. I lit up and watched him.

—Do you get it? I threw the cigarette against the student's body so that it bounced off the fleece and chipped on to the stone.

I ducked through the partial-glass door to the passage crapper.

Inside the crapper the walls were covered buff tiles embossing on to mildew grout. There was a small row of urinals and two sit-on bowl bays with saloon doors so you could see the feet if that's what you liked. Neither bolted so you had to sit with your foot against the door or else shout. I unzipped and sat down and got on the bowl putting my feet flat on the ground. I farted and waited for the bowel action. On the walls there were drawings of open cunts, birds' numbers, drug helplines for if you were buying, stories about the boy with the biggest dick in Chivermouth, smart shit-themed rhyming poemettes. Cunt for sale. Darren Dwight is a fucking poofter. Sheena goes down. I farted again and opened up my anus for the first shit to get through. I leant forward and strained, pulling in and out to let it get out. It dropped into the brown water and I got the splashes up around my retracting arse-hole. I watched the walls and strained forward again. The second shit held for a while, half in and half out. I pulled it back in and tried to cut it off with my muscles. It broke away and went in. There was no paper so I pulled up my pants, wiped on my jeans and walked past the student.

I walked back in the bar and sat down.

—Thought head and shoulders was for dandruff, I said.

—Not in the photography club, said the men.

—Got to go, I said. Uncle Septor winked.

I took the right-hand exit and pulled the door as it pushed open towards me.

Across the lamplight a shape covered my view of the bus station junction. My eyes moved over strips of purple iris flowers on long green stalks starting at a waistband and going up to a neck. The shape was blocking the doorway and smelling of soap and a triangle of light was getting in through the ankles and where the legs met at the knees and bowed outwards to the feet. I saw the silken irises and the flat face and the triangular nose turned up like a kitchen gadget and I knew the Everest hips. It was the fat girl from the Do It Easy.

Her fingers were wrapped over the dull door handle like four sausages moulded on to metal. Her chest was red and wet. Her hair was hanging downwards because that's the way hair like that went. A kid on the street was jumping up and down behind her looking for a bar, a barman, a drink. I pushed the girl back with my eyes and the kid squeezed through giving me a nod.

—It's you, the girl said.

—Yeah, I said.

—From the Do It Easy.

—Yeah.

—How are you?

—Fucking pissed off, thanks. I looked through the girl's eyes.

—Oh, what's wrong? asked the girl looking down at her waist.

—Dunno.

—Do you want to tell me?

—Eh?

—Do you want to talk?

—What the fuck are you going on about?

—You seemed happy at the Do It Easy. I mean, you seemed, you were so nice.

—I'm a happy boy.

—I wonder whose that tricycle is. The girl looked at Uncle Septor's trike parked up on the double yellow lines.

—It's my uncle's.

—Oh, is it? Sorry.

—What for?

—I'm not sure.

—Got to go.

—Well, goodbye.

—See you, love. I left and walked two miles to my house because that's where I lived.

5. Deborah Buys the Burgers

I lay awake and couldn't sleep.

It was hot and my dick was itching and it seemed like crabs and that could be Lorraine or it could be Hawley or it could be the Do It Easy crapper.

All I could think was Hawley Harvey Crippon and Alun Glenhusky together, undoing zips, rooting about, kissing the kisses of the silver screen actresses in the bus shelters of the Chivermouth wayfarers.

My bedside Awakener went. I slapped it off. It was quarter to eight.

I balanced a Danish girl secretarial student on my nose and gorged my pupils in shiny tits. I was angry, I was weak, I couldn't think or do. I felt like I was made of jelly and that I'd fall over without a rabbit shape on my back. I flicked through hand-sized magazines and wrenched my dick cruelly and coaxed softly as the sun got its way through the cartoon character curtains and Majollica crashed about downstairs with the Formica cupboards.

I got up and slung on the pair of jeans I'd torn from my sickened trunk the night before. I'd been at the cinema duplex watching an American space invasion movie where the Mars men had big heads and went along to an old crooner's stadium show to mess things up. It was a stupid movie and I'd left my brain at the door like Morgan told me only in his wit he hadn't bothered telling me to pick it up on the way out. I hadn't bothered with underpants. That happened sometimes if I was under strain. It turned out I'd left skid marks down one side of the jean seam and I had popcorn crumbs in the crotch from where I'd been scratching.

Hawley had been at the movies. I'd noticed him in the foyer purchasing a couple of buckets of popcorn, salty and unsalty. I knew he liked his unsalty. He'd had hot dogs under his arm that were squashing their mustard and onions into his sleeve. He looked like he was ready to scale an Amazonian adventure fuelled by pork junk food for two. I followed him and would have gone into a Hollywood cartoon interpretation of *The Great Escape* if Alun Glenhusky's appearance hadn't swayed Hawley's judgement towards the spacemen. I saw the back of Glenhusky, and the silhouette shape baying like a beagle at Hawley's ear by lights down was all representative of the disco reviewer. Hawley spent the jeans and hot dog adverts with his head on the shape's shoulder and by the main show he was sucking on its ear. It was mucky. They didn't see me and the clever and witty jeans advertising kept the crowd distracted but I noticed it all especially when the pair shared a King Conical double choc ice cream from the young boy vendor snaking his way up the seats in shorts. Glenhusky had a hold on Hawley I could see and it was clear he hadn't gone back to London to be any kind of father to the twins. The spacemen appeared in their flying cigar and Hawley's head disappeared down the front of his partner shape.

—Got your sausage on, Lee! Majollica shouted up the banister stairwell so it echoed on the uncovered wood stairs.

—Yeah, I said under my breath. I held my breath, stuck my tongue out and pushed my pubic hair to one side to zip up. The jeans felt damp and old from wear. I didn't care. I felt damp and old from wear.

I went downstairs holding a black singlet and sat down bare-chested at the folding shiny-top picnic table in the kitchen. I flexed my chest muscles as I pulled the milk bottle toward me and soaked the few Shreddies I felt like putting in the bowl. Majollica had the frying pan on the only ring that worked and she was turning a sausage anxiously.

—Eat up. You want to be a strong boy, don't you?

I ignored her. She was in her housecoat. She smelt of denture cleaner. The old dear came through from the garden in her short dress carrying a couple of large plastic hammers and screwdrivers the kids next door threw over the fence.

—Sports day today, Lee, the old dear said brightly.

—Yeah, I said.

—If you run like you did last year you'll have that egg and spoon race!

—Yeah, I said again. It could be any time of the decade for the old dear. She'd washed her hair and it was heavy and wet down the back of her dress where the wet had spread to form a circle between her shoulder blades.

—I've never seen anyone like my Lee go with a spoon in his hand and it's not easy, she boasted to Majollica.

—He's a fast boy, Majollica agreed. I turned the bowl up to my mouth and drank the sweet Shreddies milk from the bottom. I picked up my lunch box, stuffed it into my vinyl sports holdall and went.

The bus was full with people going to work and I was one of them. I took my place on the back seat and curled my knees up so they rested against the next back seat and I was in a foetus. I stroked my sideboards. I had a cigarette ready-rolled and I took it out and lit up. A couple of old boys with string shopping bags on their laps were talking Chivermouth. Their voices were like clouds in a damp spot of the earth. The little dry circles on the window where the raindrops had been were more interesting to me and I watched the world outside the bus through five millimetres of dust.

The bus pulled in and out of the traffic and I put my head on to the hairy seat back. From there I could watch the houses that were like mine only down bigger roads that could take a bus and I watched the garage with the morning drivers. I lived roads, streets and three roundabouts from Chivermouth centre and each one was a trial if you had a car or a motorbike but I didn't have either. I had a bus and every morning I tightened up before the boys' school.

Lorraine hadn't been at the Do It Easy for two days. Ronald said Ray had taken a nasty fall off the dry-ski slope pulley system. I said nothing. If Lorraine got me into a corner where she wanted a shag again I would just tell her to fuck off. It wasn't worth the bother, especially if I had to go down to the hospital and see Ray. I'd seen Ray once before when I was shopping for a silk shirt in Man At Homemaker. He'd dribbled over the only size fifteen and a half neck and I'd had to get orange and red instead of mauve and blue silk. I hadn't liked him. There's something wrong with you if you have deficient kids. You were of a minor race. You came from the monkeys that lived outside the main community when the human race was evolving. You weren't a man. You were a tree-house gibbon that couldn't walk without shaking. And your mother was a dried-up spinster that nobody loved.

When I reached the Do It Easy, Lorraine was back. She had black rings around her eyes. I walked past her as normal and through the plastic curtains without turning my head. At lunchtime Dear Karenza concerned herself with bursts of urine that got through when you sneezed or laughed. Ronald was subdued and slipped out, returning with two bunches of carnations and a Chocolate Orange for Ray. I smoked my roll-up alone at the green industrial skips.

In the afternoon I drove about on Ronald's ride-on delivery trolley dealing with big pieces of wood wrapped in slippery plastic that couldn't be moved easily.

—Easy goes it, Ronald saluted me as I chuffed past at six or so miles an hour holding slabs on the cart with my left hand, steering with my right.

We stocked MDF, plywood, chipboard, Conti board and all the metal kits, hinges, fascias and frames that the modern homemaker needed. We were tasteful with display. I didn't like my flat-packs leaning over and that showed. I had two gold stars and three silver on my name badge for attitude. Lorraine was grabbing her forehead and fuss-arsing her rump against the Provençal crock-pots and I was cruising past the wall brackets in reverse. I came to a halt and left the engine idling.

There was a call from customer services. Morgan needed a piece of shelving moving. The customer was at the counter as I approached. The customer was laughing with Morgan but it wasn't a problem for Claire because the customer was wearing a silken iris-design bomber jacket and there couldn't be two of them in all of Chivermouth, at least not size twenty-two or upwards.

—You following me around? I asked the fat girl when we got outside to the car park and she opened up the boot of her old model town runabout.

—No!

—What's this for?

—Displaying an exam collection of ethnic-influenced silver jewellery. I'm at the university.

—Oh, I said. They do that up there then, do they? I thought it was all pond life.

The girl laughed a big laugh and showed her tongue which was big too. She had small eyes and the lettuce-slicing lips of a tortoise, sharp and pointed like can openers or cutters that would work once you'd got through the metal. Her cheeks were full of extra fat. When she walked I heard her thighs rub together and I noticed she was wearing thick, flesh-colour tights. She leant forward to encourage the rest of her body along and she was panting by the time we got to the car.

—They do all sorts. Some pond life, it's true. Is that your name – Lee?

—Yes, I said proudly.

—And are they your achievement stars?

—Yeah. For restraining a couple of infants that got stuck together mainly. And for being a cheery boy.

—Are you feeling happier now?

—I'm always happy.

—I'm going for a burger. Would you like to come along?

—What – now, love?

—Yes, she said. Unless you can't.

Deborah Buys The Burgers

There was a drive-in burger bar for out-of-town shoppers in the car-park corner but since I worked at the Do It Easy I

86

didn't take any notice of it. I took in my own snacks and savouries. The burger bar was all-American. It was new. It was the only drive-in in Chivermouth. I'd gone for an interview and done an audition with a supervisor giving me directions from the fryer into a headpiece like I was in a pop video. I had to say the orders through a little microphone at my mouth and I shouted too loud and didn't get the job but I got unlimited burgers for half an hour afterwards for attending and in that time I got down three cod in a cob, a couple of toffee ring doughnuts and a strawberry milkshake before unfortunately vomiting with the beginnings of a head flu.

—Yeah, OK, I said to the girl. Only I haven't got any money in this, I shook the excess waist material of my romper. I'm naked under here.

—That's all right, she said. I've got some spare cash from the sale of some of my Incan items in the student union crafts corner. She reached awkwardly over the driver's seat and took up a ten pound note from a square slot in between the two front seats. It was my break time anyway.

I climbed in the front passenger seat of the runabout and bent my head down for the end of the piece of wood to be loaded. The girl slid the wood in from the back until it rested on the dashboard and she got in. As she switched on the engine and changed gear she brushed my face with the silk of her bomber jacket.

We travelled easily from the parking space over to the drive-in serving hatch. I peeped over the wood and gear stick and watched the operative speak the order through the pop star microphone. The girl nodded and handed over the cash. There was no change. We drove on to the next window and waited. Eventually a big brown paper bag came out of the window and the girl took it up and put it on her lap. The bag was smelling strongly of hamburger meat and freshly fried fries. There was steam coming out of the top. I'd had Majollica's rock cakes for lunch. The girl swung into a parking space and opened the boot to readjust the wood. I sat up.

—I expect you're a bit cramped in there, the girl said.

—Yeah.

—My name's Deborah.

—My favourite name. I ran my hand through my thick tousled hair.

—Really?

—No.

—Here, have a crack at a burger.

She rustled around and took out three or four burgers squashed into one hand and passed one over to me before reaching into the bag again to find a red punnet of fries. She handed a punnet over and we began to feed in front of the windscreen-sized world.

The girl, I noticed, made quick headway into a couple of chicken filets and went on to a triple beef. I ate slowly. She ate fast. She didn't look at the food or choose which mouthful to go for, she just opened her mouth and put the burger there then took away what wasn't between the teeth. One burger took three bites. She looked straight ahead and didn't speak or blink. Her eyes closed as the sauce got out of one side and looked like it was going to drip on to the orange polystyrene carry box. She moved the burger from near her mouth and ran the side of her index finger along her lips and then licked. As she chewed the meat and bread, she got her hands into the fries punnet and pulled out four or five fries all of the same length and she chewed her way down them in the way that a cartoon crow snacks through cartoon corn. The sausage fingers went into the bag again and this time out came a tall cardboard vat of cola with a straw in its lid. The girl took the straw in her mouth and took up a draft of cola to mix around in her mouth with the food. When the mouth was as full as it could go, all the food was put on the napkins on her lap and she swallowed. Then she got the burger up again and took bites and loaded her fingers with more fries. I looked ahead.

There were five or so burgers to get through and when I'd finished mine, she didn't offer me more. Instead I looked out of the window and listened to the sound of her mouth at work. There wasn't a lot of scenery. Behind me was the porch-entrance of the Do It Easy with a couple of wheel-along barbecue sets and a garden shed on the forecourt. Next to the Do It Easy was an electrical shop for toasters, irons, mini hi-fi and so on. You could open a budget account and spend two thousand pounds and pay it off at eight pounds a month afterwards only the interest was 33 per cent per year. I didn't go in for hire purchase. If I could afford it I bought it.

It was a small car park with a couple of dustbins and a triangular shrubbery scattered with misaimed trash. The drive-in folk thought it was a drive-in bin too and threw their brown bags in the direction of it as they squealed their brakes on the way out. That was Chivermouth. The green grit bins for the snow were full of orange polystyrene carry boxes. There were some low scratchy trees that fought off the brown bags and grew leaves halfway up the trunk. The drive-in had a small restaurant but it was often full with four-year-olds having beef burger parties where the kids ate beef burgers and played at beef burger-eating games until the burgers ran out and a young bird came out from the service hatch and made them laugh with jokes and games or one of the lads would dress up as a clown and try a bit of juggling.

All around the drive-in it was red and shiny. The frame of

the restaurant was red and shiny and so was the one-letter
sign above it to show its Scottish name although it was an
American chain and it had universities for the study of buns
and burgers in its home country. The nose of the clown was
red. The tiles on the crapper floor were red. When the new
kids got on the griddle the meat was red.

There were other cars parked in lonely spots like ours
with people snacking like we were. There were business
representatives with their passenger seats full of files and their
windows blocked with hanging jackets. There were fat lads in
fast cars like the fast cars on my estate. There was a couple
with a kiddie in a harness on the back seat and the bird was
tearing through a burger to share with the tot.

—I'm having a baby, said the girl.

I turned round to look at her.

—Is that right?

—Yes, she said.

—Oh.

—I was watching that child over there in that car.

—Uh.

—I'm only twenty.

—You're older than me, then.

—Am I?

—Yeah. I'm nineteen. Do you come from round here?

—No. She mentioned a town of couple of counties up.
She'd stopped eating. I came down to study silverware and
perfumery at the university. With my boyfriend Cedar.

—That's a fucking weird name.

—He's half-Lebanese. It's his nickname.

—Oh, I get it. Like the wood. Cedar of Lebanon.

—Yes. How would you know that?

I looked at the girl.

—I work in shelving.

—Of course you do. Anyway, he's in intensive care.

—Yeah?

—Yes. He was beaten senseless in The King's Limb on Sunday night. After I saw you. It was a freak attack. The police have nothing to go on. No-one saw anything except for my friends and they didn't really notice anything until Cedar went outside with a boy and that was it. I'm overcome. I have to be strong.

—Jesus fuck. That's too bad. He was half-Lebanese, then, this bloke of yours?

—Yes. He looked English and didn't have an accent when he talked or anything but he was born in Lebanon.

—Well, that's just too fucking bad, that is.

—Yes. You're very sympathetic, Lee.

—What does he look like then, your Cedar?

—Oh, he has dark hair. Sort of a quiff style, I suppose. He was in the back passage for half an hour.

—No!

The girl was wiping her mouth with napkins and I could see pale orange stains on the paper from the sauce round her mouth.

—Too fucking bad, I said again. Deborah, do you believe in fucking weird things happening to you and that?

—Coincidence? Do you mean fate?

—Dunno. Like, fucking weird things happening to you and that.

—Yes. No. I don't know. Mine's a pretty hands-on degree.

—Oh, I see. Well, then. Better go.

I climbed out of the girl's car and walked back over the car park to the Do It Easy. I passed by my photograph in the store entrance and stopped to admire the lighting technique the young bird photographer had used to make me look a very good-looking boy.

Lorraine was leaning on the customer services counter running her hand over the wood grain as I stepped inside. She wasn't strictly allowed to roam the store. Morgan and Claire were standing together looking like they meant whatever they were saying. They were a happy couple and they liked to hang round the older ones.

—One minute he was strapped on tight and the next he'd slipped through the safety bar, Lorraine was saying as she wrung her knuckles on the counter top. Claire was shuddering and looking very closely at Lorraine to give sympathy.

—Morgan likes to keep it clear round here, I said to Lorraine as I got shoulder to shoulder with her. I wiped down the counter with my hand to remove her knuckles.

—Fancy a coffee, Lee? Lorraine asked eagerly as I turned to go back to the ride-on.

—Got work to do, I said and went off towards the end of the store. Claire and Morgan shrugged and divided for their departments.

—Go on. We can't just leave it after the other day. Lorraine followed me, talking to me.

—What other day? I asked with hollow eyes in a style I'd practised.

—It won't do any good to keep it all inside.

I reached the ride-on and got into the driver seat, flashing my rompered buttocks at Lorraine's face. She carried on looking. I drove off down the aisle in the direction of plastic storage. She ran after me.

—Meet me in kitchens, I shouted.

I parked and dismounted the ride-on, flapping my way through the plastic curtain. I hoisted at my romper and got over to where Lorraine was standing fiddling with the belly of a misplaced U-bend. She was in Tuscany Morning, a pale red and green Formica four-piece cut-to-fit with a double stainless steel sink and gold tap accessories. I checked the cupboard under the sink stand. It was empty of Lorraine's sales aids so I told her to get inside. She was standing around expecting something and she looked at me when I said it.

—Get in there, then.

—What for? she laughed.

—I'll show you.

It was late afternoon and quiet on the floor. The people who wanted kitchens had bought them and the people that wanted help could use Morgan. Lorraine looked around, squatted down and crawled in through the double doors.

—Leave it open a bit.

I unzipped my romper.

—You're a randy cow, Lorraine Sweet, I said and got it so my front was across the door opening.

—What are you doing? she asked as I pulled my dick free from my pants.

—You want it, don't you? She laughed. Just fucking swallow it, then. I don't want to lose my job.

I held the front of my romper together and eased my groin to where Lorraine's open mouth was waiting behind the doors. I swelled up as I felt her hold my dick between her teeth and wet her lips where she could.

—Ungh, she grunted, trying to make the swallow.

She moved forward on her hands and knees. I pushed my hips forward and my balls reached her chin. She started to move back and forth, sucking while she could and I stood still looking around the store from over the sink top.

Apart from a small kid and his father mixing and matching

in doorknobs, the Do It Easy was empty and I started to rock slowly forwards into the doors. I looked down and saw that Lorraine had her legs open under the interior sink fitting and she had her hand working away at her satin knickers, one finger pushing the cloth off.

—Faster, Lorraine, I said. I got confident and pushed back on my feet then shafted in to her face. She was dribbling down one side of her face. I could see the film of saliva over her chin and my balls were wet, the protective hair sticking together. I lifted my head and looked into the distance half-looking for staff or customers, half-gazing sightless at the grey ventilation bars swinging off the ceiling. I stopped short for Claire making her way about with time sheets.

—No Lorraine, then? said Claire, leaning against the sink stand, separated only by Formica from Lorraine hunching over my dick.

—She's around somewhere, I said, breathless, stopping, mouthing the words.

—I think she likes you.

—I'm spoken for, I said, panting.

—New girlfriend?

—Yeah. Blonde.

—She'll be upset.

—She'll swallow it.

Claire looked at me.

—Oh well, then, Lee. See you later.

Claire headed off back to the office above the shop floor. Lorraine started going at it fast. She'd got her legs up into triangles against the doorflaps. I jutted in, held and pulled out. We sped up and I breathed as much as I could under the hot strip lights.

I pasted Lorraine's mouth over. She coughed and sucked. I

pulled out and wiped my dick against her sleeveless cardigan. She swallowed. I zipped up.

—See you later, love, I said and made for the plastic curtain on weak legs. I didn't look behind and I didn't see her get out or straighten up.

6. The Photography Club

The sun was getting down in the sky by the time I stepped into Chubby's for a cone of chips and a turkey on a stick.

Little Chubby Junior was frying at the back of the shop under a curled picture of sea fish and plants done by the primary over the road. The picture was stuck on beige tiles that were the same colour as the stainless steel vat of lard Little Chubby Junior had out on the fryer top. It was six o'clock and Chubby's was roaring with orders. Little Chubby Junior was flinging bread-coated spam behind slide-open glass, dipping cod and plaice in batter, and ripping plastic coverings off frozen pizzas for the microwave.

—What's it to be then, Lee?

Little Chubby Junior's assistant Delia popped up from under the counter with a handful of salad cream sachets. I'd nearly fathered Delia a kid until she'd given in and got down the clinic.

—Turkey on a stick and a small one, please, love.

—A small one? She was a girl, Delia.

—You know what I mean.

—I know what you mean.

—All right. Make it a large one, then.

Little Chubby Junior looked at me over the frying stand. He lowered a wire basket into hot oil at his side and the oil rushed and bubbled around the chips noisily so I had to speak up.

—Make it a large one, I shouted. Delia took the money and I stepped aside, nodding over at Little Chubby Junior.

Delia reached forward into the frying stand and pulled a peak of chips toward her with her scraper. She exchanged for a shovel, took up a portionful and slipped them by their own grease into a thin card cone. She propped the cone against the till and squirted vinegar on to the steaming pile. The vinegar didn't stick and it ran off the chips. Delia shook salt over. They weren't for me. I watched Little Chubby Junior pull a turkey on a stick out of the freezer behind him and he separated one from a cluster with his hands. He threw it from where he was into the hot oil and it started up more noise. I turned back to the front of the shop. A kid got in and pumped some twenty pence pieces into the fruit machine so it gobbled when he pressed the three big buttons. The buttons pressed easily making you want to press them more. I knew. I'd lost money to it before.

Little Chubby Junior had introduced a jukebox to Chubby's and a ledge where you could stand and eat. You could put your own salt and vinegar on if you stood at the ledge but it was five pence more for each order as Little

Chubby Junior or Delia had to clear up after you. You got chip forks. It was fair. The jukebox played what was current for the kids and it was working its way through an English band with a cheeky boy singer. The band liked to sing about England and its ways like getting the car bonnets up on Sunday mornings and going to your local bar with the boys and shagging the birds in Ibiza. I didn't mind them. They didn't do me any harm. The boy singer wore a thick bead necklace which wasn't necessary and it looked like he'd been surfing or something but he had a way of making the words sound electrified by using his tongue on his mouth top like he had a lisp.

I looked outside on to the scene. The housing association had the old folks home on their corner which was fair seeing as they got maintained better than the council houses. The housing association was tidier than our road. There wasn't so much activity. There were regular houses just before the old folks home but we didn't see the regular kids come out of the regular homes. Some of the regular homeowners didn't want the old people's home when it was only plans so the council offered them a nutters day centre instead and then they wanted the old folks.

You didn't see the old folks. Most of them sat in a double-glazed porch area on hard settees watching a small TV or using a little plastic watering can on the nearest house plants along the window ledge. Some of them wrote letters on their laps or sat in their high-backed chairs and watched you go past. I didn't mind them unless they waved you in with their skinny finger and called you son and asked you to post a letter for ten pence. They got confused. The box was right there next to them if they just got up out of their chairs and stepped outside. Most of them could live alone, they'd just given up. Some of the men were randy types and they made a grab for the old dears on the bench on the grassy tussock by the entrance sign.

Chubby's chip shop was the gateway to the estate that was Surrey Housing. In the other direction you came to the primary and the roundabout and the garage that sold to a video shop when no-one wanted to run it as a garage so the pumps were dead and the oil and antifreeze shelves got filled up with film boxes. Over the park was the boys' school. Down from the park was the Pizza Warehouse and Richard's Hair Office and then more shops with flats over the top. You couldn't get chips in the Pizza Warehouse. It was for people who wanted to sit down for junk food and be served it by a young kid in round glasses. All you could get was pizza and salad and red wine. I'd never been in. Richard's Hair Office had been Ricky's Top Stop until Richard's Hair Office sounded more like it was in the 1990s. It was the same man and the same haircut only more expensive. I didn't bother with it. I went to Hair By Sidney's little loft on the Barbican and had a shave at the same time.

Little Chubby Junior was giving me the eye from his side of the frying stand. It was nothing to worry about. He'd been showing Delia the saveloy for a couple of months now. The turkey stick was ready. I took salt and vinegar on the chips and headed off down my road.

The kids' toys were on the road by the evening so the cars had to swerve and some kids were still out in the dark pushing themselves along with their feet and waists. I passed an upturned tractor and avoided a torn pushchair sized for carrying a twenty-four-inch or so toy toddler. It was a toddler's toy toddler chair.

I got to Uncle Septor's and saw the windows covered in dark material from the inside. The windows were blacked but there was music. The music was a rocky guitar sound, the sound of 70s and 80s band Stay The Same where the men wore long hair and patched-up denims and they sang along together and covered the hits of other artists. They were Uncle Septor's favourite band. I recognized it from his car stereo casette collection. Stay The Same Gold – All The Hits And More. Philharmonia Plays Stay The Same. They were played at all the weddings. They were timeless.

Further up Majollica had the cocktail nuts on the barbecue trolley and Richard was relaxing with her on a folding chair. They both had glasses in their hands and Majollica was holding a gold plastic telescopic cigarette holder. I'd seen the holder before at Uncle Septor's fortieth birthday street party. Majollica had got drunk and slid it back and forth in my face all evening. Now she waved it at me and shouted my name. I nodded. Richard curled his toes in the uncut grass as he relaxed and one of the estate cats got around the leg of the folding chair pressing its cheek against the tubular metal.

The old dear's shape was in the window as I walked past. She heard the door and came out of the lounge. There wasn't room for two so I got up on the first stair.

—I got the egg and spoon race, Wendy, I said and she didn't understand.

I stepped indoors and got down two plates from the dimple glass-fronted kitchen cabinet. I unrolled the paper of chips and turkey stick and shared them out over the plates. A turkey stick was a piece of meat shaped into a turkey bird and stuck on to a wooden stick. Chubby's did curry-coat versions and deep-fried bread-coat but I liked regular and so did the old dear. I took the plates into the lounge on a slippery rose-design tray and put them on the poof. I bought in orange squash in a beaker and a can of lager for me. The old dear switched on the telly and we watched a game show where you spun a wheel and won prizes. I brought through a bottle of ketchup and turned it upside down to let the sauce run down the side. I put it on the floor up against the settee. I cut up the old dear's turkey stick and she started into her chips. I started to eat mine with the lager.

—Need a bit of sauce there, Wendy? I asked the old dear.

—No, ta, son, she answered.

The fat bloke from Wales won all the prizes. It was ten to seven. I kissed the old dear on her red cheek and got upstairs to change into a pair of glossy football shorts. I put on the black singlet I'd worn that day, rubbing a squirt of aftershave into the thicker neck seam before I put it over my head. I had a reasonable tan which faded where sleeves would normally go but that was just normal with singlets. The shorts covered tan-fade round my arse. I had pants on underneath but the shorts had a white net liner of their own in case you didn't want to wear pants at all. I was easy with the stairs and I took them two at a time through experience of my own house. I pulled my leather jacket off the ground-floor stair post and stepped outside.

I nodded at Richard and Majollica spearheading their own shadows under the street light and passed Uncle Septor's house on the same side.

Deborah was already outside Chubby's as I swung round the top of my road.

—Hallo, Lee.

—Just got to wait for someone.

—One of your friends?

—Relative.

Deborah was wearing the silk bomber jacket and a different skirt with big flowers on. She was in a tunic with a low oval-shape neck and covered buttons of the same material down the front. She had the tights on and I could hear her legs as she moved from one spot to the next so she stood still.

—Won't be long. I nodded at Chubby's. Ever eaten out of here?

—No. It's a bit too far for me.

—Oh, you live around the university, then do you?

—Yes, I'm in halls. It looks very nice though.

—You'd enjoy it.

—I'm sure I would.

—Like a bit of a fry-up, do you?

—Yes. Sometimes I like a nice crunchy vegetable.

—But not often, eh?

—No.

I leant my back against the shop window and kicked the base of Chubby's brickwork with my black trainer.

—You'd make a good advert for this place if you stood there like that all day.

—Would I? she said. You know, I was thinking about what you said earlier and I thought how sweet you were to help me and be so sympathetic about Cedar when you don't even know me.

—I'm a nice boy, Deborah.

—Call me Debbie.

—Hokey cokey, Debbie.

Uncle Septor came round the same corner I'd appeared from and he made his way over in swaying slacks and stiff black slip-ons. He pretended to duck down like a boxer on the defence as a greeting and he put his fists up to me as he got close.

—Watcha, Lee, boy, he said, tapping my arm and turning to Deborah. Who's this lovely lady, then?

—This is Debbie from the university. This is my Uncle

Septor. He lives round the corner. He sort of looks after me after my dad did a runner.

—Hallo, said Deborah.

—Hallo, girl, said Uncle Septor.

—Uncle Septor runs the photography club round here.

Uncle Septor looked at Deborah.

—You're interested in photography are you, then, Debbie?

—Er, I suppose so, yes. I haven't given it much thought. I'm a creative person.

—Debbie's a student at the university. She makes jewellery.

—Yes.

—But she's a bit upset and needs cheering up at the moment because her Lebanese student boyfriend got done over in The King's Limb on the weekend and now he's in intensive care.

—Strewth. That's a shame, love. People'll do anything these days. Don't you worry. You'll be fine with us. Confidential venue, see? Keep things exclusive.

Uncle Septor winked at Deborah and guided her back down our road towards the estate and the confidential venue which was always Uncle Septor's house with people arriving staggered throughout the evening.

Uncle Septor's housekeeper Alison opened the door to us. Alison was a sixth-form student at the grammar. She was catering for the evening and opened the door at the end of the redbrick tunnel with a plateful of bitesize sausage rolls. Deborah took the plate.

—I'll be mum, she said.

As we stepped into the dark hallway, Alison came back with cheese and pineapple on sticks. She led us into the front room and I could see why it was so dark in Uncle Septor's house.

Uncle Septor's ground floor was made up of a big lounge. He didn't have a diner or a kitchen. He had a kitchenette through a beady curtain. He'd knocked the walls out himself. It was his own design. He had installed a concertina-fold divide which was pressed back against the walls but you knew if it was unfolded you would have two rooms. The windows were covered with dark curtains which were tacked on to surrounding wood batons. The curtains were lined with heavy pale brown material and they hung down on to the floor making lumps of excess cloth. I hadn't seen the insides of the curtains before. Uncle Septor nodded at them as I looked about.

—Chivermouth Operatic Players' curtains, they are. House curtains. Last used in The Mikado, 1979. See that, Deborah?

—Were you a Player, Mr Trebilcock? Deborah asked with the natural inquisitiveness of a jewellery and perfumery student.

—No, love. Stepped in to retrieve the damage after an arson attack on the Players' town hall lean-to. Before your time. It was a long-running strife between them and the Tae Kwon Do class over town hall bookings. The Players lost their lean-to and the Tae Kwon Do got Tuesday and Thursday nights. Most of the costumes went. Curtains were so thick they got damp. I took them and a technicolour dreamcoat of the same thickness. Never caught the man that did it.

Deborah sat down on one of sixteen or so canvas and metal chairs and she closed her legs as shut as they would allow. I'd watched a nasty documentary about fat people with a blonde bird having her stomach stapled and it showed the operation with the doctor forcing his hand in a glove through bright yellow fat to get to the dry pale mauve stomach to get his staple gun in. Three or four men had to hold the fat aside for the doctor and even then he was puffing. Deborah took up some spicy ribs with her spare hand and started chewing down their sides without looking.

The chairs in Uncle Septor's lounge were lined up like wartime chairs. They were the type you folded but they weren't like Richard and Majollica's floral chairs. They were functional from a batch of many hundreds that once filled all the halls in all the country while the bombs were taking out the coastal towns.

I was used to the green decor of Uncle Septor's lounge. He'd taken down the pictures for the evening and put up a display of photographs of mob football match violence set in Italy with men in painted faces and uniform T-shirts running towards the camera waving pieces of wood. The men in front were clear and their tongues were crisp on the paper. There were men on the ground being beaten round the back and sides by men with bricks. The men were curled up with their hands on their heads. There was a man walking away holding his head and you could see blood. There were a couple of panoramics of crowds herding outside an Italian stadium while the Italian coppers were joining arms and flashing see-through shields into the sunlight on the edge of a wasteland building site.

The pictures ran along the wall to the kitchenette where there was a painting of a jackboot on a face and the jackboot had a swastika on the side where the ankle would be. It wasn't real. It was a painting.

—Club trip to Milan that was, said Uncle Septor. And that, he pointed at the jackboot, that was our Auschwitz fortnight. Hope you don't mind the lads and their football, Deborah?

—No, said Deborah and she didn't because Alison had left a plate of chicken drummers near her.

I rolled a smoke and pulled the tobacco threads out of one end of the fag so I didn't end up chewing it and getting it stuck in my teeth. Uncle Septor's was a grown-up house. He didn't have dolls on his mantelpiece. Alison passed by with a tray of plastic cups and I took one, waiting for the ale that would fill it up. I took a trek to the far wall and had a look at the Africans being tied up and electrocuted with cattle-prodding sticks in a honey light.

—Burnt sienna filter used on that lens, said Uncle Septor on the way over to the door. I recognized the Club Climax in one of the black and white pictures. There was a scene of a razor blade running over a face with a figure that looked fast on his feet and a homosexual that was dropping to the floor.

—Evening, Septor Trebilcock.

It was Reg's voice in the hallway.

Reg stepped into Uncle Septor's lounge like an astronaut boarding a capsule, stepping carefully over an imaginary height on the threshold. It was Reg's way to dramatize what was happening at the time and create some mystery around himself. The room went into hush and that was only Deborah, me and the bird Alison ushering about with a three-litre economy ale bottle. Reg stood aside from the chairs and rolled his fag from a plastic pouch of Bullmaker's Golden. Uncle Septor moved about the room straightening pictures and snapshots, Deborah held a paper plate with quiche so that the plate folded in the middle with the weight and Alison turned the neck of the ale bottle on herself quietly in the corner. I stood in my shorts and singlet, hands pushed into my leather jacket, thin cigarette stuck to the edge of my mouth. My hair was tousled so as to be attractive and my chin was starting the seven thirty p.m. growth of a man. My brown eyes were thick with their own colour, I knew that. I knew the behaviour of my eyes when I was waiting. My face was like a spruced cocktail peanut waiting for the silver shaker. Reg came over. He spoke into my face.

—There's no replacing Reg in this club, Reg said in a lowered voice.

—No, I said, equally lowered.

—You did all right Sunday night. Want to get out tonight and see a bit?

—Maybe.

I looked over at Deborah massaging her calf.

—It'll be mostly candid work . . . as-it-happens . . . point and shoot . . . know what I mean?

—Yeah.

—It's a big one. The Chinese Open All Hours.

—Do they?

—Then after that a quick trip up Nut Avenue to let our friends with the coloured skins know they're not welcome outside the house in daylight hours. Get it?

—Yeah.

—Hear you've got a subject in mind of your own.

—Maybe.

—Young lad been at your trouser leg, is it?

I looked away from Reg and over to the projection screen which was blasting a pale blank square in the electric bulb light.

—Yeah.

—Who's the bird?

Reg nodded his head towards Deborah.

—Girlfriend of the kid on Sunday night.

—You're getting a bit sharp, aren't you? What – does she want some too?

We turned together to look at Deborah. She was scratching one hand with the other. She was sitting up straight to improve scratching.

—Dunno.

Gradually the other chairs filled up with young men arriving. The men wore short haircuts and long donkey jackets. One of them brought in a bulldog and made it sit down at his feet. The bulldog was female and wouldn't sit. The man kicked the dog and it did. We felt more powerful and the room relaxed up. Uncle Septor started up his projector. Alison got the lights and we sat and watched our smoke cover the credits of a short Nazi propaganda film about the harmful effects of tolerance on society and the contrasting effects of a sole powerful race. Uncle Septor spoke the translation from pieces of paper. The film was old. The figures walked too fast and the movements were clipped so that a raised hand suddenly went down or a kiddie stood up without kneeling or bending. It wasn't like real life. It was mainly family life in the picture and the kids had special outfits to wear for the club they were in. They were keen kids it was easy to see and they had mothers and fathers that weren't absent or barking bonkers. It was a nice time in history it was plain to see. There certainly wasn't any room for boys in dresses.

Uncle Septor ran the story of a woman who was awarded two party medals for dedication to the blond race for providing four white-haired baby boys.

There were riot scenes after that and pictures of Indian men in India and Indian men in English corner shops. There was jungle footage of monkey and gorilla communities and black people on Cassandra Way and Nut Avenue who were treating Chivermouth like it was their home. Finally there were pictures of men holding hands and kissing and pictures of a group of men breaking it up with lengths of wood nailed with screws and tacks. The big bald man with the thick glasses from The King's Limb sat down next to me.

—Just finished my dinner, he whispered.

Uncle Septor winched up a new-model audio-quality television on a telescopic stand in front of us. He took the remote control handset from the shirt pocket under his cardigan and programmed it with autumn twig fingers. He had some home footage of a petrol bomb attack on a Pakistani cigarette-seller in a kiosk near the Chivermouth Royal Theatre. It was simple procedure with a man in a khaki Ford Cortina pulling up on double yellow lines and putting a milk bottle across a counter on to papers stacked on the floor at the back of the wood hut. The footage had been edited afterwards and there were three or four cameras at work.

One of the young men had made a soundtrack with church hymns playing 'Jerusalem' and a voice-over saying that there were two million unemployed young men in England who could do the cigarette-sellers' jobs and that the two million young men were English white men who should expect a living from their country. The voice-over said the cigarette-seller may be open eighteen hours a day when most people wanted to get home for dinner but there was no reason to give the jobs to the Pakistanis when we could do it just as well. It also said the cigarette-seller was locked into the kiosk by the proprietor in case of burglary or assault from the side door. Uncle Septor told the men who made the footage that they'd made a sensitive piece of film for the photography club and that it might even be sent away to a national organization. Uncle Septor said he some-times got secret newsletters from the national organization. Uncle Septor said we would break for Alison's Battenberg cake.

I approached Deborah on the chairs in the break and sat down next to her with my shorts up on my thighs.

—Are you sure this is about photography? she asked, ignoring my hands astride my hairy trunks.

—Yeah, I said, yawning, kicking the chair of the big bald man.

—Do you think it's got anything to do with Cedar?

—Your Cedar? He's in intensive care. How's he going to bother us from there?

—No. It's not that. I don't know. It doesn't feel right.

—That'll be your birthing hormones.

—It's only been two months.

—Deborah, I rolled my eyes, I brought you here to cheer you up. I didn't have to.

—I know. And it's very nice of you. But, well, they could have killed that kiosk attendant.

—As far as I know it was first-degree burns.

—You're a nice boy. I know I'm stuck into my jewellery and natural scent extractions but, well, I just don't know.

I looked at her sideways.

—I live at number 51. My old dear's got Alzheimer's. In case she doesn't know who I am. If you call.

—Oh, you poor thing.

She put her hand on mine and I crunched her fingers from below.

—Lee, I'm scared after that attack.

—Eh?

—Why did they do it?

—He was a student, wasn't he?

—I'm a student.

—Probably because he was a twat. I'll walk you to the park. There's a hopper stop the other side.

She passed through the door sideways.

—Why do you like me, Lee? she asked, as I pointed out my house on the other side of the road.

—Dunno.

—You could have any girl, couldn't you?

—Yeah, probably.

—Why me, then?

—I'm a bit confused with my best friend Hawley trying to turn me into a homosexual.

We were at the park edge. Deborah stopped and turned to me. The park was quiet. The street lighting had been on all day where the council got the times wrong. The grass went to mud along the tarmac path and the shrubbery bushes lay on their sides like scale-model dinosaur skeletons.

—Over here, I said so Deborah would be confident with the way we were going. I walked on ahead to the Red Indian lookout. Deborah caught up and panted. She stood in the mud dip where the rain and trash collected.

I jumped on to the lowest telegraph pole and started to walk around getting higher. I looked down at Deborah's wedge shape struggling to stay up.

—Bet you go at it like a steam train, Debbie, I said, watching the thin hair crown rotate to find my voice. She turned to follow and look up at me. She looked fatter from where I was, ten feet above her. I could see her round shoulders and the way her arms lay on top of her sides instead of against them.

—I've never shagged a fat girl.

She looked down at her flat shoes. She fiddled with the zip of her silken bomber jacket, the silken bomber jacket that would never close.

I stepped along the telegraph poles and turned on the last so I was fifteen feet above her.

—We're all animals.

She stood in the centre of the lookout where the grass was rubbed away to mud and where the puddle formed after rain. She put her head down.

I jumped off the tallest pole and fell forward on my hands. I put my knuckles on the mud floor and walked on my hands and feet like a monkey.

—What do you need the fat for?

I put my face to her belly walls.

—I don't.

—It's for the pain.

—It's hereditary.

—It's fucking obese.

—It's glandular! she cried and I knocked her to the ground.

I lunged at Deborah and pulled her down into the mud. I knew the Sumo girl would stay in the ring. I took the waistband of her silken bomber jacket and pulled it off her back. The sleeves caught on her wrists. She fell on to one arm for balance. I pulled her up by the tunic and forced the jacket off the hands and dropped them on the floor. The tunic was slippery. I could smell Deborah sweating and I could smell the smell of her cunt that was sweat and daily lubrication. Deborah was on her knees. I took off my leather jacket like there was a movie on the telly I'd always wanted to watch and it was starting. I was kneeling and I pulled the tunic until I felt it hurt Deborah and she cried. Deborah didn't cry out. She cried tears that started with one and went on to two, three and four. She was crying. The tunic tore under the arm and I kept pulling. I took up the slack with my teeth and ripped away from the areas of resistance like the seams and buttons. The tunic came away and Deborah showed me her bra which was big and reinforced. Deborah's skirt was elasticated round the waist and I pulled it down so fast she fell forward so I could get the material around her knees. I threw the skirt in the air towards the highest pole. Deborah was wearing thick flesh-coloured tights and high-waister white pants with thick cuffs around the leg. Then she wore another pair of pants that were beige skin colour and the pants had special elastic for holding the figure in. I tore away at the tights and pants until the tights laddered and the pants came down. Her flesh resisted like meat in an abattoir that exists because it is dead and not because it has any life properties. I saw the rolls around the tops of the thighs, each starting where the last left off. The rolls weren't equal on either leg. One had seven or eight and the other had nine or ten so they didn't balance or fit together. Deborah's arse hung by gravity down on to the jelly skin. The arse was flat but wide, wide as two of me. The waist hung forward so I could never have seen the cunt hair. The tits were like long-dead rabbits in specialized carry sacks. The arms tried to pull into the body sides and the body sides tried to pull in the arms. I didn't get up. I pulled down my shorts and pants. I took off my singlet over one shoulder and pulled it down the other. I turned Deborah round with both arms like rolling away the stone. Rolling away the stone and finding Jesus is gone.

'And did those feet in anci-ent times walk up-on England's pastures green.'

She rolled around and I pointed my dick in her face. My dick looked small, oiled, as misshapen as Deborah's mutation body. I poked my dick into her eyes and nose and ears. I pushed it in her ear and started fucking her ear and then I fucked her eyes and her nose and I pushed it again and again in Deborah's face and I picked up her hands and put them around the base and she held my dick and I pushed it up and down her face and I heard Uncle Septor's trike at the park entrance and I looked up for the moon and the moon wasn't there and the sky was black like night is supposed to be and the shrubs lay about exhausted like nobody wanted them and Deborah held my dick and I fucked her face and I worked back and forth in a rhythm and I came over Deborah's face and she closed her eyes.

7. The Camera Is a Plumb Line Released Off a Picture Rail in a Derelict House

Deborah twitches her leg and says she has a cramp in her shin and I move my knee off her thigh and her leg reshapes. Deborah is on the ground. Deborah is holding me tight. Deborah with fat girl's asthma and hardened arteries and sleep apnoea. Deborah forgetting to breathe. Deborah with protein semen in the corner of her eyes where the sleep dust dries. Deborah crying. Deborah sighing.

I look up at the half-ring of sawn-off telegraph poles that make up the lookout and I watch the thick grain under the creosote of the trees cut to use-size. The poles grow together towards the black sky and if they carry on growing they will meet in the middle.

Deborah lies nude on her side, legs like rock-climber ledges, feet useless steamer paddles on fleshy ankle stubs. Her calves shape like athletes' steroid calves with swellings under the bone that smash on to the mud. Her thighs join regionally at the cunt and hold together the foothill ridges of her gristly leadweight excess legs. Her cunt holds me into it but I didn't have my dick in her. I am lying outside her, inside her, inside her fat. My legs are angular on her land-mass hips, my back straight down the middle of her polystyrene-packing belly. Her mattress waist spreads over the mud like a gentleman's cloak on a puddle. Her nipples flatten out like saucers either side of my shoulders and her arms get around my back like marshmallow girders. Deborah's face sticking to mine with semen. Deborah's face saying 'ssshh', 'ssshhh', 'ssshhh'. Deborah's fingers in my hair and in my sideboards and in my mouth. Sausages in my ears, sausages in my coiled chest hair, sausages on my mind.

There's a kid in a womb that's turning with the way the mother's positioned herself for knitting the bootees and the mother's got chocolate piping sauce under her fingernails and the father's got a short glass of brown ale on the settee arm and the TV is switched on to Television South West and the mother and father are watching 'Police Detective 604 Precinct' in black and white. And there are fried onions stuck in the sink plug and slices of bread on the garden floor for the birds which never come and the mother gets the pains and gets the hospital bed and gets the baby blues in the afternoon and the father gets up and closes the door like he'll always be back and slowly the baby gets down off the settee to get holding on to the mother's apron hem and the mother can't remember what November 1st 1943 is and it's her birthday.

The camera that is my life starts at the star that isn't above my head and it speeds through the cosmos like a Star Trek opening scene and it finds the earth like a magnet. The camera is a fork sinking in water. The camera is a plumb line released off a picture rail in a derelict house. The camera gets over the smoky orb Earth with its plasticine peaks and oil-painted oceans and smoky lines of clinging cloud and it turns corners with itself to get to land-masses and shapes and lights, little Christmas tree lights of humans together. The camera dips over the doorstep of the universe through the cloud layer and the night and the winking lines of the coastal city that's held on the island by crust and tidal habit, past the exhausted sea that can't see you and can't wave, past the tiny cliffs with their wrist cuffs of seafront esplanades, past the stone stairs and the male naturist observation points and the worn-out naval constructions, past the statues of yesterday's no-name heroes saving yesterday from the day before, past the skinny plinth hotels standing up like ball-less dicks, over the vacant flat building tops, over the coiled rail track aslumber half out of glass and metal awning, over the dry-bed green parks with the bulbous-head trees and nervous rash borders, past the garage that's a video shop with antifreeze titles to warm your cock hearts, past Chubby's chip shop exhaling vegetable oil air like a life smoker, down the white lines of my cul-de-sac, scraping its carriage on the white lines down my road, through the bollards that say 'don't drive here it's for dog walkers'. The houses and streets grow like cutdown forest shadow and the camera comes to the bouncy chickens and the shitpeak pooper sign and the castle remains and the Red Indian lookout that's green in orange light. There's a human mass in the middle of the earth fitting and unfitting like granite moor rocks that have been pushing up through the crust of the earth. Unpeeled in shit and naked on chip forks, bare and skinless in a half-circle, exposed to the castle remains and the sheepskin jacket dog walkers and the sleek heavy-chain collar dogs, half-circled by telegraph poles, pissed upon, licking semen off my eyelids while the swings hang on the top bar too high for any kid to reach, Deborah is eating me.

Deborah holds me close, so close, like a baby, like voluntary strangulation. Deborah holds me under the wood poles of the Red Indian lookout and she puts her fat around me and keeps me warm. I want to die all the deaths I can die while Deborah's fat arms squeeze me into the shorts in the mud and I shiver so cold in March. Never let me go, Deborah, I say while the night-time rats and voles get out for their civilized hour of gnawing on whatever stands still long enough. And the dogs come by and sniff at me, all over me, stopping, sniffing all over me but Deborah just holds me closer.

8. The Chinese Open All Hours

I kick away the singlet and shorts into the mud and press them further in with my foot. I wipe away the mud tears and peel off the dry semen from my cheek. I hear Uncle Septor idling the trike engine at the entrance to the bollards.

—You ready, Lee?

I heard him shout across the orange street light.

—Yeah, I said from the lookout. I put my leather jacket on and pulled it across my chest. I walked to the park edge in trainers and white socks. Uncle Septor had parked the trike and was revving the engine with one wrist.

—What's happened to you?

—Nothing. Got to get dressed.

I walked into the house and up the stairs. I dressed into jeans and an imitation purple Italian design sweatshirt. I put the leather jacket back on.

I swung up alongside Uncle Septor on the trike as he twisted his wrist around the handlebar, commanding the engine. The buggy wheels worked into reverse and the trike manoeuvred against the four concrete posts of the park path. Uncle Septor straddled over the white lines in the road and we rode out slowly.

The low handlebars pulled Uncle Septor's legs forward so he was almost lying. He was a warhorse warrior with all the time of the undefeated. The lights moved from amber and green before we needed brakes. The night cats walked against the tyres under the stationary cars. The fog got up around the orange street lamps like ghosts that wanted revenge on the steel poles. The streets were washed with day damp. Uncle Septor lay along the trike under his wrist playing ten o'clock lamplight sonata on three gears.

It was dark. There was no moon and there were no stars. There was a fog over Chivermouth. It was cold, the sort of cold to get in your bones for ever. There was a wrapping round the earth. I kept my fingers along the back of the seat and felt the pain before the numb. Uncle Septor took the roundabouts and filtered left and right over the lanes, sliding over the road in motion. Chivermouth was made of round-abouts that kept you going around until you realized you weren't getting anywhere and you were just going round and round.

The centre of Chivermouth was for pedestrians and it had a covered arcade of shops as well as three lines of streets of the same shops. Before Chivermouth had got pedestrianized, the main car park was to one side of the shopping centre so you had to cross a road to get down in. You could drive all around and wait for a meter or you could park up and be near. When you had crossed the road there was a shop selling sewing material and further down, the army offices for joining up. The army offices were like a shop and they had lifesize models of men in the window using guns or cooking food or using radio systems. After the pedestrianization, the army offices stayed but the sewing shop sold up to a high-street building society. The car park got flattened for a walkway and the flower beds read Welcome To Chivermouth in crocuses. There was a new car park in a sealed building right next to the old site and there was a supermarket to go with it. The Chinese Open All Hours was opposite the new car park between the army offices, the building society and Harry G's bar on the right side. It had always been there.

You could filter off the main roundabout for Chivermouth rail station or circle the car park. The road circling the car park was where all the shops had their back doors and it was written up so Harry G's had HARRY G's on the rear for deliveries and parking, the army had SERVICES RE-CRUITMENT and so on. The circular road was always littered like a New York cop scene with blowing newspapers, trash and low, fast, expensive cars that were nicked, refitted or two or three years past the registration plate number. It was the nearest Chivermouth would ever get to New York and it was where the underground organized crime went on. There was a Balti curry house where all the suits got in to discuss and the flats above ran with birds' first names on the intercom like Cherry and Farrah Full Massage. The Chinese Open All Hours was the only store to open from the back and it had a ramp to go down while you were selecting.

Uncle Septor made a turn into the rear of the store. He followed the empty road held in by the walls of the army offices and the high-street building society. There was no fog in the rear of the Chinese Open All Hours. The scene was as clear and as big as Screen One at the duplex. Uncle Septor stopped the trike and climbed off holding the handlebars.

I followed him around the back of the trike. He made room for himself, sighed out of his lungs and stretched forward his hands to loosen his arms. He shook his fingers and jogged on the spot in the stiff slip-ons then he reached down each of his sides to work his hips.

—Got to be ready, son. Warm yourself up a bit, then.

Uncle Septor stood before the banana boxes and slid out a wooden bat and a machete that was out of the constabulary weapons amnesty bin. I took the bat and swung a couple of times in the road. He passed me a red handkerchief and I tied it over my face. It had been the fashion two years before.

Reg and two kids came down the car-park ramp with bats in their hands. The kids were eighteen or so, brown-haired but the hair was short so the scars showed. They had brown eyes and mouths that if they spoke would have said 'what are you looking at' and I was looking at them. They were simple bats they were carrying, from a simple sports shop, sold for baseball or field rounders. One of the kids had a camera slung over his neck and shoulder so it was tucked into the crook of his arm for safety. Uncle Septor cut the air with the machete only the air didn't cut. Reg rolled a Bullmaker's Golden and put it between his lips so they locked on to it. The kid opened up the back of the camera and fed a film on to a spool. He clicked the door shut and wound the film on until the first frame was ready to go. Reg nodded.

—This is Stevie. Reg pointed out the young man with the camera. That's Mick. Stevie's got the camera.

Stevie was slimmer than Mick. Mick was six foot or so with a wide chest and tight blue jeans so his gut hung over. Mick was in a black leather blouson jacket with a grey-collared tennis T-shirt underneath. Both were in heavy black lace-up boots. Stevie was scrawnier with bad skin and teeth that stuck forward except for the front two that stuck back so he looked like a vampire in reverse. He was in a green shiny bomber jacket and a black T-shirt. I was in jeans and a purple sweatshirt out of the *Homemaker*. Uncle Septor put a woolly hat on my head and I pulled it down over my forehead.

—Get round the front, Barnardo boy, Reg told Mick. Mick got round the front. Reg swung the back door open. He stood in front holding Stevie back with his hand on Stevie's chest. Reg moved forward down the ramp, tapping the bat up and down on his free hand. Stevie moved to the left and I followed Uncle Septor down through.

Mick came through the front door and shut it behind him. I stepped out from behind Uncle Septor. There was a pimply Chinese kid of seventeen or so reading a book flattened to the counter by his hand. The kid looked up and you could see that his eyes were full of the Chinese thriller or history or romance because he didn't register anything in the pupils. Mick stepped forward and hit the counter with his bat.

—Lock the door, Mick said into the kid's face and the kid shook up and got out from behind the counter.

—Lock the fucking door, you dozy fucking Chink, Mick said. The kid got to the door and closed it up at the top and bottom but his hands were shaking. He wasn't ready for it.

Reg guided the kid to the end of the store with his bat and the kid slunk down around the tin stacks lining the ramp. Reg turned to us and used the bat to signal.

Mick ran his bat along the top shelf starting at the front window. We stepped back and he went along the lower shelf, smacking the packets open. Stevie got around and started to snap the camera. The kid shrunk down and Reg took up his bat and swung it around him at the shelves then he moved and swung again.

Mick and Reg stood swinging their bats and the packets and jars in the store came off the shelves and smashed liquids and dried foods into stacks so you slid to get anywhere. Uncle Septor got his hand down the freezers and followed the electric cable to the mains and he hacked through. The shelves hung off each other and fell into the food.

The kid ducked down low and Uncle Septor took a swing at him with the machete so his hand got caught. The kid screamed. Stevie got around and got the picture on his camera. The kid was screaming and the family got down out of their flat with their little rice bowls and they saw the kid's hand and they started screaming too and Uncle Septor took my bat and started swinging at them one by one as they came down so they caught it on the side of the head and went down with it into a stack. The little old men and women at the end tried to climb back up the steps but Reg caught their ankles with his bat and they fell on to the steps and came back down.

Mick had a spray can under his jacket and he sprayed around the walls. I swung the bat behind the counter and smashed the till open until I could take the notes.

—Leave the money, Reg said. Dirty fucking Chink money.

Stevie wound the film, took it out, slipped it in his inside pocket and reloaded. He got on his knees and got in the faces of the little kids on the floor.

—Need a fucking flash for this.

—Please, no, said the proprietor. Please no. Mick swung at him with the bat and he went sideways with it. The women screamed. The young kid sat with his legs wide in front of him, his cut wrist in one hand, holding the hand on to the arm. The blood was pumping on to the dried food. The young kid's eyes were climbing out of his head and he was screaming and shuffling along the floor like a rat had eaten the hand off. Reg walked about with his bat and brought down the light bulbs. He nodded and we turned to go.

Outside, Reg, Mick and Stevie walked up the car-park ramp and Uncle Septor and I put the bat and machete into the banana boxes and got on the trike. Uncle Septor looked up the car-park ramp and then turned the trike round.

Uncle Septor joined the traffic at the rail station round-about and fed into the stream. He drove at regular speed up the main drag on to the Barbican and we cruised over the sea front and felt the air. Uncle Septor did gentle wheelies along the quiet road and he stopped so we could look out to the sea and see the island named after a seaman. We saw the lights but we didn't see where land began or ended.

—My home, Uncle Septor turned and shouted. This is where I live, son.

We turned and joined the Unity Street turn, feeding in along the arrows in the road. The clubs in Unity Street were open and the take-out bars were working through pizzas and chicken parts. Strings of birds with elastic legs worked arm-in-arm down the pavement, little handbags jiggling on hips and white arses, crotch-length dresses shaping over hot unwashed bodies and underwire bras. Kids in hunting packs swung glass beer bottles at where they knew their mouth was. One time there would have been sailors of all nationalities crossing the pavements but now the dockyards were closed and the naval bases turned into open-plan flats and girls' schools. But the birds worked on and the pimps got out of bed at eight or so to get them out there. Sex wasn't a commodity like the chicken quarters. Sex was the breath on the out take. If you breathed in, you breathed out. You had to put it somewhere, into something. The birds were working with the rhythm of lungs on Chivermouth.

Unity Street started where the shops and the entertainment centre stopped. It had been so that you didn't want to drive up it for the birds on the kerbs and the kids in uniforms getting out of their everyday discipline. Now there was a kids' store where Unity Street began so you walked over a steel and glass corridor to get from the car park to the kids' store and you looked over the chewing-gum rails and saw down into the street which your mother didn't want you in. Trash along the pavements and all-day bars. Trash up the walls of the theatrehouse club and trash in the doorways of the hardware shops behind their night-time iron curtains. Clubs where you could get in and watch a show – a couple of birds with a plastic snake or two. Bars where you could get a beer and get a middle-aged crotch ground in your face. Clubs like Slammers where all the red balls from the pool room had been nicked or Sahara Nick's where the birds were in bikinis for the start and they danced on a podium and you got put out on the street if you tried handling them. Bars like the Eagle where the scarheads got in all day and fought each other across the roads while the cabs didn't bother swerving.

There were eyes everywhere in Unity Street. Eyes staring out from glass cabinets of cheap chicken quarters being crated into paper boxes, eyes flicking out of black cabs for a fare, eyes over bow ties giving you the nod from the club doors, single eyes flashing out of the thighs of the dresses of the birds on night duty. Out of Unity Street there were old eyes, eyes in bodies in old dresses and new shoes, eyes in flaky make-up that wouldn't stay on the lids, eyes over Majollica elephant-tits, old birds on roundabouts swinging one leg, old birds swinging used, dried cunts on to yellow lines while the kids tuned the bonnet-up racers in the lay-bys.

Uncle Septor got off the street into the rear of the British Albion bar. He stopped and turned the engine off. He undid his jacket and took out his rolling tin. He opened it up and took out two ready-rolled cigarettes. He lit one and gave the other to me. I drew on mine and sat back.

—Come on then, he said and took the trike keys out of the ignition.

In the bar, Uncle Septor ordered American whiskies and we sat in the back until an old bird came over on black heels in a black dress. The dress used the bird like a skin uses bones and you could see the paunch where the old bird had had breakfast fourteen hours before only this wasn't the type of bird to eat breakfast unless it was live and wriggling.

Uncle Septor talked to the bird and put his whiskey down his neck. There were other birds in the bar talking round the pool table and at the bar, hanging down low in low-cut dresses. Uncle Septor winked at me and I followed the bird outside the bar and down an alley past a closed skating rink. The bird got up into the housing at the back of Unity Street and we rode up two floors in a lift with dented doors, piss floors and spray walls. The bird got out and opened up a door next to a blue wood frame porthole. I followed the bird into a regular lounge with a two-piece Dralon suite, TV, mini hi-fi and kid's cot. The kid was asleep. The bird moved into the corridor and opened the crapper door to show me then she opened the door to a room with a single bed, sheet, cabinet, bowl of water and used towel. There were magazines and a picture cutout of a cunt and an anus on the panelling. That was to get you going in case you got there and weren't in your stride. You could sit quietly and get worked up over the snaps.

The bird closed the door and stepped out of her shoes so she was lower than me. She sat down on the bed and bounced a little, tapping the bed beside her, looking at me.

—Come on, love, she said, picking up my jeans hem with her stocking toes. She tried to pull me to her but she couldn't hold the jeans in her toes. I moved anyway and stuck my groin into her face. She undid my belt and pulled the jeans down to my knees, pulling first one side away, then the other. My dick was limp and curled up. The bird used her nails to pick it up and she looked at me as she started to squeeze it lightly by the base. My dick jumped. I held my sweatshirt up to my chin with one hand. I pushed my pubic hair down with the other. The bird began sliding my dick with her fingers slowly in and out until it got big enough for her to use her hand. She pulled it back and forth and then slid it to her mouth where she held it on her brown lips raising her eyebrows at me. I shoved against her and she was off-balance for a second but she got back and opened her mouth. She took my dick and pulled me in and out of her by my arse. I looked away from the bird and at the picture cutout on the darkstain fake wood panelling. The bird used her mouth like a cunt and I stood still. The kid shouted. It must have been two or three. It used words, the words it used for its old dear. The bird carried on pulling me in and out. I yanked my dick out, bashing her lips. I was hard.

—How much?

—Septor's got it covered. Come on, love. Healthy boy like you.

The bird tried to fondle my dick again but I grasped her wrist in my hand and twisted. The bird jumped back and took her arm away. I got back in my jeans and zipped carefully.

—That's for the kid.

I look out a couple of notes I had shoved down into my jeans.

—Not good enough, then?

The bird kicked one leg towards me. I got out of the flat and joined Uncle Septor in the bar.

—That was quick.

—I'm a quick boy.

Uncle Septor put another whiskey down his neck.

Nut Avenue was past Unity Street. It was a small road twisting its way up from one main road to another. It was the thoroughfare to little roads that went off it and made little worlds of Jews, Blacks and the Indians. They all lived together packed in a vacuum flask of their own natural heat. They didn't stray and there weren't many but there was a line and once you were over it you knew someone was watching you. You got to Nut Avenue through a one-way system past a scratch of green where the Indian kids got out and tried to play cricket in the summer. The little birds were always hanging off the walls in Nut Avenue. They would be on their bikes, leaning against the road sign, twisting the wheels with their ankles, looking up into the sky when you got by. The older kids would be leaning their bodies against the sign and walls, arses squashed into shiny flared trousers, nub tits in gold button tops. The boys got around the girls like they needed protection, hanging round in baseball caps, empty faces, a job to be done and that was to give you the eye, the nod of warning. I see you. I know you're there. The boys sat on bikes, curling round on the seats, never getting off, falling over and getting up, wearing heavy sweat tops, vacant leather pistol holders strapped to their shoulders ready for the day when firearms got the better of the police forces. The older kids hung around the entrance to the flats, maybe crowding round an uncle in a topless sports car with a bass box playing jungle like a nuclear plant thumping to make the tree stumps shake. The black kids owned the entrance to Nut Avenue and the black kids were hard. Further up the road were the Jews that lived in the basements like underground cities with their Jew relatives and Jew tenants and busy Jew lives that meant they couldn't see you coming except to cross over the street and get away back to their busy Jew day. The Indians lived next to the Jews. The Indian kids stood on their own cardboard by their own trash with their thin hair wound into buns on their heads, their trousers falling off their arses, dresses too big. The Indians' friends turned up in big German cars and sat outside and stared until no-one was there then they went inside and you smelt the samosas. The Jewesses bought a warehouse where they cooked for all the Jews in Nut Avenue and Cassandra Way. You always smelt the Jew food coming out and when you passed by you looked through the broken basement windows and saw the dark-haired women mixing their bowls and bread. The Indians had bought two houses and joined them together and they educated their kids in Hinduism after their school day.

Nut Avenue was council buildings and private houses where the windows were boarded up with chipboard and painted black and the kitchen sinks were all over the pavement. There was always cardboard and rotting TV chairs or tenants' possessions across the road. The adults kept inside and got out into their little gardens at the back where a dog or two lived tied up and barking all night. I knew all about Nut Avenue. You could get an eighth of a herbal ounce to smoke in the long afternoons and get under the tree with the rest of the kids on the green scratch and smoke till you slept for a few minutes but that was enough to put you out of the game if you were adult. I didn't bother with it.

At night, there was always a band of police cars round the one-way system, wailing to get by so all the traffic had to get on the kerb. There was always a car or so parked up on the lines with a black kid on the pavement shrugging his arms or standing in the ready position for arrest which was skulking unsure but knowing. The police didn't get up into Nut Avenue. They preferred to do their work outside of it and pick up whatever came through. They pulled you over for your documents whatever your colour. Nothing stood out in Nut Avenue. Uncle Septor pulled up after a black German car.

The air was different in Nut Avenue. It was warmer. It was tropical. This was tropical Chivermouth. The stench of the foods hung around the air long after the act was over. The figures that came out of the houses had a reason for living. They were living so they didn't die. We climbed off the trike between two tree stumps with small green leaf sprout. A kid locked a derelict house and stared away from us as if to say 'I know you're there' and we were.

—Leave the trike here, said Uncle Septor, it'll put them off. Put this up your jumper.

He handed me some jump leads attached to a small battery. I held them against my stomach and spat on one of the tree stumps. Uncle Septor put a junior baseball bat up the sleeve of his jacket, slid a small thin packet of razor blades into his breast pocket and slung a small silver-case tourist camera round his shoulder.

We walked down through Nut Avenue to the one-way system and followed the road back to a strip of twenty-four-hour shops – videos, kebabs, off-licence. Uncle Septor said it was the best way to get them, when they weren't expecting it and when they weren't near their darkie mates. I walked alongside him, waiting for the nod. Uncle Septor went into the off-licence and leant on the counter top with his head level with a round, flat loaf of bread. He licked his middle finger and brushed the flour off the bread with it. He looked up at the Indian owner.

—All right, mate?

—What do you want?

The Indian was dressed expensively in a woolly jacket and violet-shade glasses. He was standing over the till holding cash money. There was a skinny Indian next to him looking like he was getting a nappy change.

—What is it? the Indian owner asked again, pushing the cash into a blue bank bag, signalling the assistant to take the till over.

—Got something for us?

The Indian pulled at Uncle Septor's sleeve to drag him over towards the cold beers. He spoke low.

—Last time was the last time.

The Indian didn't sound matey. He sounded scared. I stood behind Uncle Septor and reached in the fridge for a beer. I snapped the top off a Cooler and poured it down my neck through the inconvenient tin opening all the beer cans had.

—Inflation, said Uncle Septor and lunged into the Indian's face to breathe on him.

—I'm trying to run a business, said the Indian.

—What do you think *I'm* doing? This is my assistant, here Uncle Septor put his arm round my shoulder. I need co-llat-er-al. He said it slowly for the Indian to understand.

—I can't afford it any longer.

—You'd better think about it, Ranjit—

—It's Sangit.

—You'd better start thinking, Ranjit, because I need paying round this time of the month. I'll take that for now. Uncle Septor took the blue bank bag and put it into his trouser pocket so he had a bulge there.

—See this? Uncle Septor lifted his arm and poked the junior bat at the Indian's face. I don't carry this around for home comforts. Get it? The Indian nodded and Uncle Septor nodded at me. We left.

—See what I mean, son? Thick as fucking pigs. Thick as fucking pavements. That's why we walk on them. Place would be running with the fuckers if it wasn't for us. Here – get a snap of that face.

Uncle Septor handed me the point-and-shoot silver-case camera and I aimed at the off-licence window. The Indian was looking out at us. I snapped, wound on, repositioned, snapped, wound on. Uncle Septor tensed. Along the shop front a black kid was coming out of a late-open record store.

The way that black kids walked was to show you they'd gone past regular rhythm they were so fucking cool. Like they would lurch and bend, doubling and trebling the beat of the walk or go off on the down beat. It was all to do with the jungle rhythms. You saw it on the movies with the black star saving the airplane crew in disaster or being a Los Angeles cop. They had a way of bending and lurching and turning one foot to get along just to show they can do it.

This kid was bending and lurching out of the store past the reggae music record sleeves of rubadub sounds and Jamaican duo singers playing calypso. He was cruising down the strip like it wasn't today and he was heading for the coconut seller on the beach and the sunshine over the crab boats but it was Chivermouth and it was the night. The kid was alone and looking up like the black kids did. They looked up. They didn't look you in the face. Too ashamed that they were on your doorstep without good reason. Uncle Septor nodded. We fell in step, two paces behind, and listened to the kid singing under his breath a street beat he'd got in his head in the record store. The kid turned into a small street off the strip and squeezed past No Parking bollards. Uncle Septor stepped up and put his hand on the black kid's hood. The black kid stopped and looked round. He got sight of Uncle Septor's grey stubble face and asked the question with his eyes so we saw the custard whites. Yes was the answer but Uncle Septor didn't speak. He pulled the kid's hood so the kid had to run backwards to keep up with him. The kid was sixteen or so, in glasses like a studious type of kid. I helped drag him into the turn of a garage lock-up where you could get around to a quiet area of tyres and dead batteries.

—We've got a message for you and your darkie mates, Uncle Septor said as the kid stopped using his legs and let his body go loose so the hood started to rip with his body weight.

—Hey, hey, leave me alone, man. I'm not doing any harm.

The kid scuffed his trainers on the uneven concrete to get standing up.

—Don't you fucking try it.

Uncle Septor cracked the kid one on the head with his junior baseball bat and the kid went down. He lifted the kid's head and held it with one hand. He took the glasses off by unhooking first one ear then the next and he put them so he could tread on them at some time later.

Uncle Septor held the kid's head back and moved the black eyes around with his fingers like he was looking for something. He squeezed the eye sockets and made the eyes jump around. He looked inside.

—See that? See a darkie jump? Nothing in there.

I got out the jump leads.

—Not doing any harm? said Uncle Septor. The harm you're doing is bringing this country down to your fucking monkey level with your filthy fucking ways, my boy, he said. Can't seem to teach you. You've been getting out of your houses in daylight hours again. You're harming the fucking kids round here with your darkie ways.

The kid breathed loudly as I got the leads plugged into the chubby battery. He started fidgeting and trying to get free so I pushed him down on to a raised manhole cover so his back went up against the propped slide-door panel of a Transit. The panel slipped and the kid slipped too.

The leads were attached and I put one on the kid's ear and one on his tongue while he was shouting on the ground. Uncle Septor held his hands and legs. The kid was shouting and the metal was clanking against his teeth and he was nearly swallowing the lead. I switched on at the battery and the kid's tongue went black and hissed. His ear shook. I switched off. Uncle Septor got out the junior baseball bat again and gave the kid a good tap in the mouth and on the ear. The kid tried to vomit with the lead filling up his mouth.

—Got my fucking hands dirty on your nigger fucking hairstyle, Uncle Septor said.

—Dirty cunt, I said and kicked the kid in the stomach three times taking a run-up. I rolled the kid over with one foot and ran to the back wall of the redbrick private area. I turned round and ran back up to the kid to kick him in the sides and back.

—This is my assistant, said Uncle Septor. You've got to be nice to him.

The kid was on the floor in the dirt of day-to-day car maintenance. He wasn't curled up in a ball with his legs over his stomach and his hands weren't on his bead. He was looking up at us like a fucking little git and he was asking for it.

—Don't you come around here with your fucking coconut food and reggae music.

—Lee. It's me. Darkie Jim from school.

It was like a dream. The kid was looking up with his tongue swelling with blood.

—What's that?

Uncle Septor was getting ready with the razor blades.

—Darkie Jim. Remember? My brother Saul. You know, man.

The kid was swallowing on his own blood. I pulled the lead off the tongue to get it clearer.

—You mean, I know you?

I made sure.

—Yeah, the kid spluttered, dribbling.

—Put your tongue out. Go on. It'll help things along.

The kid stuck his tongue out and I kicked his chin so he bit the tongue. I ran against the wall and took two steps up it like a gymnast. I turned on the redbrick and ran back and got the kid in the ribs then I ran back up the wall and got him in the mouth and he groaned and sighed and Uncle Septor held his forehead taut and I scratched a freehand NIGGER with the razor blade so the blood filled up the eyebrows and the skin stuck up like cut tree bark and the brown face was running with red blood just like mine only mine was where it should be, in its veins, and this kid's was getting out all over the concrete and screws and stray springs from the garage day.

—That's it, son, said Uncle Septor.

—Merely personal, Darkie Jim. Hold it there, will you.

The kid lay on one side like he was hurt in the feelings. I stepped over and waited for the red flash indicator to come on. I got as close as I needed to express the moment and snapped.

—Fucking 'nigger' on his head!

Uncle Septor looked away in the direction of the trike.

—Got to look after your own.

I turned my head back at right angles to my backbone and laughed so loudly they heard it in the mud huts of Africa.

—Ha ha, I laughed. Ha ha ha.

9. Hawley Gets the Warning

—Look, Hawley, I may as well tell you, mate, there are people in Chivermouth that don't like what you are and that's a fact.

—I thought I'd never see you again, blubbed Hawley into his stone face pack.

I twisted my thumb nail into his chest.

—That feels nice.

—Christ, you're a pervert.

Hawley Harvey was lying on the Posturepedic with a Dead Sea mud mask on his neck and shoulders. He was in shorts. Eric and Elsa were naturist caravanning in the Lakes in a two-birth tow from the caravan rental on the Chivermouth bypass.

—I do mean powerful people, Hawley.

Hawley wriggled down into the counterpane and squealed.

—You scare me, Lee. I've had Alun here all over the weekend and my gums are sore. He's so exciting but I'd give him up for you. You know that night, Lee. On the couch at your place. I didn't think I would ever feel like that. I felt ooh so weak in your hands. All the time teen tenting and I never knew. You'll make a boy very happy.

—Shut the fuck up, you little pervert. I've just come round to warn you to watch out. My family's into stuff and people get hurt. Things are changing. I'm taking control of my life. I'm making my own decisions now. I've met someone.

—Oh.

Hawley's clay face went still and his hands dropped away from his crotch where he'd been playing about like a little kid at bedtime.

—Yeah. It's a girl. A big, fat girl. I mean, I don't know what's going to happen. She's huge and I've seen her naked at the Red Indian lookout. I've had her, Hawley, in the park. It's having a big fucking effect on me. I don't want you to get hurt but things are boiling up and the people don't like it.

Deborah was on my mind and I didn't need the banana-straddling Swedish student secretary in the morning to tell me she wasn't. It wasn't so much the grip of the arms or the weight on my limbs that left my muscles dead and crying for oxygen to pass through. It was Deborah on her knees in the earth circle crying and holding me close to her that had got me to thinking and to having mercy on Darkie Jim and Hawley Harvey.

—What are you saying, Lee?

—I'm saying I want this bird to mother my child and that you're going to get your fucking legs broken one day soon either this week or the next.

—Not me, Lee. Nothing ever happens to me. Except

for Alun and Elwood's court appearances.

—Well, it fucking will and you've been told now.

I was driving my nail into the embossed wallpaper Hawley had seen fit to paste on his walls. I'd already had the corner off his Singapore monkey-design treasure chest that was on the floor where I'd been kicking in time with my warnings. I could smell my own dead piss from last time and it was mixing with the Dead Sea mask and Hawley's violet-scent drawer liners.

—You know I've pissed all over your underwear, Hawley. I spoke so low he wouldn't hear.

—Alun wants us to adopt the twins and live in a sunny garden flat in Chivermouth.

—His bird's not going to like that. It's fucking painful having kids you know, Hawley. I know. I went through our Ferd's process. You've got to get the milk going before you can do anything. It's a fucking hideous show.

—What's that, Lee?

—The milk. Oh fuck, I don't know.

—She understands Alun. She'll come too. It'll work.

—Oh Christ.

Hawley reached over the counterpane and poured cold water on to his mouth.

—I'm hot.

—I might need a godfather, I said. Look this isn't a joke. I'm in with some powerful people now and all I've got to do is say the word and your balls fry in Crisp 'n' Dry.

—Sounds nice.

—You're fucking bonkers just like your old woman.

Hawley rubbed his chest and sighed. His little dick was half-awake in his soft material beach shorts.

—I'm sorry, Lee, he said. I'm just so pleased to see you. I do like you, you know.

—Fucking shut up. I've told you now. When are Elsa and Eric due back from camp bonkers?

—One week. Alun's coming round and I think he's going to take me to London with him in his boot. It looks like his girlfriend is happy with two actively sexual fathers for the children and I've always wanted to have children. Alun knows a Tibetan who runs a class for simulated childbirth pain experience so you can identify and relate. It sounds right for me.

—Identify and relate? They're the weaker fucking sex.

I looked down at Hawley's pebble eyes circling in the green mask. Dead Sea was right for Hawley. His skin was clammy and wet like the ugly North Sea fishes that turned up in the fish shops once a year. He'd lost the pink prawn horns and the big black filmy eyes and the spiky whiskers but he was still the flat fish flopping around on the big deck. His hand fell on to the turntable of the Dansette Bermuda player where he'd spent the afternoon with a Mario Lanza long player. He caught his thumb on the chunky stylus and lowered on to the chorus of 'You Do Something To Me' for a second. I scratched it off.

—You're cruel, said Hawley with his hands back making a tent of his shorts.

Over the room were his clothes, female label leggings, nylon slip petticoats, a suede-look Cilla Black jacket from the 1960s, a Parisian jumble sale green dress suit with a hand-written label, hard denim button-fly jeans, the rock star shirt. The chest of drawers was covered in half-burnt candle stubs in eggcups. The dowel collection rack of botany-theme porcelain thimbles from the last century was snowed over with talcum powder and a packet of three Matey Ones Tuff was jammed in the door frame.

I sighed.

—Hawley, you are going to die.

—Oh so what if I am? he cried after me as I took the stairs two at a time through experience of that house too. So what? I've seen happiness and it's in your trousers.

I got to the bottom of the stairs, heard the last and jumped back up the stairs. I slammed through the hollow flammable door, found the bed with my leg fronts and grabbed Hawley off it by the skin of the neck. I lifted his head holding him by one thumb at the larynx.

—You don't get it, do you? I snarled. I'm in control now. I make the fucking rules.

Hawley winced.

—So what, he squeezed out in a high voice through my thumb being positioned on his voicebox.

—So what? he squeaked.

—So. You're a fucking pervert, a coward and a bully.

—Alun will protect me. I'm not scared.

—Alun Glenhusky wants his big dick up your little arse. He doesn't want to look after you.

—That's not true. Hawley started crying. I'll kill myself if it's true.

—It's true.

I exited the lounge of Hawley's housing association house with 'do do that voodoo that you do so well' playing with my mind. The springtime flowers were getting ready to open their buds along the little lawns spread apart by tarmac pathways. The daffodils grew like weeds along the pavement and the mauve crocuses were lying down on their sides with the force of the breeze. Hawley's house was just like the rest of them, it just had more space round it than mine. The Crippons had a breakfast bar and a panelled lounge and a sun lounger patio on concrete at the back. They had a double slide door for going outside and a slope up the front path for approach. They had a drive and a garage and a little alley to other housing association homes which had the same white wood front Lego block sections between the top and bottom windows. The Crippons were semi-detached.

I got to the old folks home and didn't bother looking in.

In my road the pants and pyjama bottoms were clipped along the plastic ropes on the front grass for the once-a-week airing. One of the kids had a ghetto blaster on the pavement and other kids were crouched round it planning, their little white chests in four-pack kiddy Woolworth singlets. Little tiny birds were nursing dirty plastic children along the low home-divider walls that stood for nothing. The little birds had little bottles that emptied when you held them in the plastic babies' mouths and went full when you turned them back up. The little birds were dressed up in pink and turquoise snap-together jewellery and tight Terylene shorts that showed their T-shirts and cheap knickers round the back. Kids didn't feel the cold. Kids didn't feel anything. I couldn't remember being a kid.

I dodged the fancy footwork toddlers as they side-stepped the cracks in the pavement. I flung on to my house past Majollica, past Richard, past Wendy in the double window pressing a plastic geranium into a plastic pot with her plastic fingers. I pushed the concrete bollards of the park entrance aside with all the strength of both arms but they didn't move. I ran across the half-inch grass and mud dried into shoe shapes. I stopped at the half-surround of the Red Indian lookout and pressed my body against the highest telegraph pole to look up to see it against the sky. I fell down into the circle of dark moist earth and Opal Fruit wrappings and bottle lids and I spread out on to the thin ground as if I could feel the next layer of the earth below the crust under my skin.

I felt the bone of the earth under my back like a hard elbow that juts out when someone's on the telephone and they think they're alone. I felt the hardness of the earth, how hard it was to lie on it, how there was no comfort and no big belly to run to. I curled into a foetus and tried to remember Deborah under me, holding me up, telling me to be quiet. I screamed silently with the pain from my stomach to my lungs. The kids, daytime dogs, came over and sniffed at me. They stood in little clusters and came and looked at my face, angling their thirty-six-inch bodies to measure me by the eyes. I barked at the daytime dogs and they ran away back to the bouncy chickens and the tyre swings. It didn't matter. It didn't matter any more. The earth was an elbow in a long phone call when you couldn't get by the cramped nook. They could unwind the top layer, slip me in and leave me there. It didn't matter.

Uncle Septor was in the front room watching a video of two kids and a Shetland foal on a picnic rug on the Dover clifftops. He had freeze-framed the Shetland's dick and it hung static near the static snogging kids. Alison was in the kitchenette making meringue nests and I wandered through the beady curtain to find a beer. She passed a lager tin from the icebox and wiped fridge mist off the circular top.

—He's had the police force round, Alison said quietly as she cracked eggs open and stood shells against the sink edge. They've placed him at The King's Limb when there was some violence.

—Not him.

—It's all right, she said, beating the eggs and looking straight ahead at the black wheelbarrows on the wall tiles. He's in the clear.

—Oh.

—They might want to speak to you.

—Yeah, maybe. What's all this for? I was looking at sugar going in to a big bowl.

—Oh, I'm a girl guide. A leader. It's for a jamboree in a copse near Budleigh Salterton. They love nests.

—Uh.

Alison stood on one leg.

—I think that's why your Uncle Septor and I get on. I think I understand him and his needs. He told me all about it.

I joined her on one leg, leaning against the door frame with my body.

—About what?

—What happened to him in the navy. His experience. I do understand him.

—Oh. What experience?

—Are you all right?

—Yeah. I think I want to get close with a girl and I'm not sure about stuff, that's all.

—Don't be scared to let it out. We haven't really talked, have we?

I looked at her.

—Eh?

—I'm a good listener.

I knew Alison was a good shag and that she had good vaginal wall muscles which made all the difference but I was suddenly tired.

—Dunno. Got to talk to Uncle Septor.

I went out of the kitchenette. Uncle Septor was in front of the juddering freeze-frame white cliffs scene. His leg was up on the settee and he had a tin of beer in his hand. There was a cardboard box of videos on the floor next to him.

—All right are you then, son?

He didn't look up.

—Yeah, I said to the back of his head.

—What about your fruit-flavoured mate? Better sort him out while we're thinking of it.

—Yeah.

—Next week sometime. I need something to release me up a bit as it is. Feeling a bit stressed. You know we've had the coppers round?

—Yeah.

—They seem to reckon I've been down at The King's Limb of late. Alison sorted them out. I was here with my Shetland dick. Just got the channel over to cartoons in time. Don't want them sniffing round that. What have you been up to then?

—Nothing.

—Next week's best for the poof. All right with you?

—Yeah. His folks are away caravanning.

I looked to Uncle Septor's neck and hairline. His head bobbed as he spoke to the TV screen.

—Is that a fact?

—Yeah.

—Well, that's convenient.

—Flammable doors in that house.

—Flammable doors! Flammable house. Leave it with me.

—Fancy some snacks? Alison shouted from the kitchenette.

—Ta, I said and edged back towards the kitchenette. She passed out bacon strips in a breakfast bowl. Uncle Septor was rewinding the tape with the paper over his lap. He was leaning forward carefully. I went back to the kitchenette.

—What's this about my Uncle Septor, then?

—What do you mean?

Alison was shaping the nests on paper to go in the oven. Her fingers worked quickly but she looked up and flashed me with her grey eyes. Alison was a nice bird if you liked housewife types that kept you organized. I peered closer to her crochet tank top tits and leant my back down the door post like a sexy cat. I breathed out. Uncle Septor had got

Alison from the sixth-form college. She was taking a religion A level.

—What's all this about the navy? I said again.

—You know that your uncle was released with throat trouble.

—Yeah. Years ago. Before I was born.

—Well, it was a special kind of throat trouble.

—So?

—It was throatal gonorrhoea.

—Eh, that's what birds fucking get.

—I'm worried about him.

—I'm worried about you. You're the fucking housekeeper, Alison Lunch!

—He'll only give it to me in the rectum with a pillow under my tummy for support.

—What do you mean? You're a fucking tart then!

—No, Lee. I understand him.

Alison's fingers didn't move from the white nests she was building on the paper. She kept her eyes on the meringue walls as if she was commanding them to rise up and walk.

—My Uncle Septor was all over the world until his sickness.

—Yes, he was. Alison paused and jutted her head down on to her chest towards the nests. He was very upset when they let him go. They didn't like him handling the food. They have very high standards in their galleys. I'm scared something terrible is going to happen. I think it's all coming back up again. I don't think his family helped. He lost his wife Brenda. She fell in love with someone else.

—Yeah. A darkie insurance salesman that crept around in the dark like a darkie would.

—His brother Frank wasn't happy about it.

—That's my dad you're talking about!

—I know. But Septor loves you and that's why he doesn't want to talk about it.

I looked through at Uncle Septor with his hands under the paper. He shouted through for Alison to bring in another can and Alison looked at me with the kind of look that says 'this look says it all' but I didn't know what it all was except that Uncle Septor had got his merchant navy papers with a tickly throat and Alison took it in the arse on a rubber support pillow.

Alison put a kettle under the tap. She held the kettle and tap together. She turned the hot tap on and the water splashed against the sides and caught on the stainless steel. The water tank above the sink roared and the gas flame jumped. Alison looked at the inside of the kettle. The nests were away in their oven. I looked at the black wheelbarrows on the wall tiles.

A kid was loading up with the Shetland on the white cliffs of Dover. I wasn't staying. I gave a parting glance to the back of Uncle Septor's head dipped over his torso and got into the hall. I twisted the lock with a professional-size football in my throat.

Uncle Septor's little black shiny gate held me in so I kicked my way through, loosening hinges, swearing.

Wendy was in our hall with a piece of paper written in Majollica's tangly hand. I took the paper upstairs and slammed the crapper door. I wrenched down my jeans, straddled the bowl and worked through the curly balloon letters. Lorraine had phoned. She was putting forward a case of sexual harassment to Pete. I farted and the door chime rang out 'Auld Lang Syne'.

I pulled up my jeans and looked down through the iron window bars to the road. There was a small panda car on the kerb outside the house. It could be for any person in any house but I sensed it was for me. I checked in the sink mirror for skin irregularities and went down the stairs.

Wendy was in the lounge with a WPC and a plain-clothes copper. From the look, the copper didn't care much clotheswise and the WPC didn't care weightwise. He was in checked trousers with a hound's-tooth design and she was out of shape. Together they made an imperfect couple. I hesitated outside the door. They were giving the old dear the quiz.

—Is he here, Mrs Trebilcock?

—It's about Frank, isn't it?

—Lee Trebilcock. Would that be your son?

—It's about Frank! You've found him. You've found who did it!

The WPC was trying again.

—We need to ask your son some questions, Mrs Trebilcock.

—He's dead.

—Your son's dead?

They were cracking on now.

—Frank's dead. Someone took him.

—Why don't you sit down, said the WPC, patting the settee and nodding to the copper. The WPC sat down next to the old dear.

—Could you tell me again? the WPC asked the old dear.

—It's my Frank. Someone took him. I think they've killed him. Haven't you found him yet?

—Oh I'm sorry, Mrs Trebilcock. When did this happen? I wasn't aware.

—Yesterday. He didn't come back for his fish bites. I had them all ready. I had them all cooked. Lee was in his pyjamas. He was ready for bed. His dad read him a story sometimes.

—How old is your son, Mrs Trebilcock?

—Six.

—Is that your only son?

—Yes.

—I think we've made a mistake. We were told your son was grown-up. We wanted to ask him some questions about an incident in which a student was attacked.

—Not my Lee. He doesn't fight. The only time they sent him home was when he was chasing the girls round the playground and they didn't like it.

—We must have made a mistake. Do you have friends or neighbours we could call on for you?

—My brother-in-law Septor in number eight. He's very helpful but Frank and him don't get on.

—Number eight.

The WPC nodded at the copper and the copper stood up. He came over.

—Who are you then? the copper said to me as he got to the door.

—Leave her alone, I said.

—All right, all right, said the copper. You Lee Trebilcock?

—Yeah. She's got Alzheimer's She's confused. Leave her alone.

The WPC stood up. The copper stood across the lounge doorway.

—We've got to talk to you. The copper looked me up and down. Down the station.

—I'm busy.

—No you're not, said the copper. The WPC stepped out. The copper jerked his head into the lounge and I went.

—She said you're only six, the copper said. The old dear had got her forefinger into her dress hem and was twisting the material around.

—She was thinking of when my dad ran off.

—When was that?

—1983. October 12th.

—So he wasn't murdered for his fish bites then?

—No.

—Shame. We were going to reopen the case.

—There was no case.

—We could start one.

—You could start anything.

—Now, now. Get your coat.

—I've got my coat.

—Get in the panda then.

I went over to the old dear where she was sitting deep in the scratched vinyl settee.

—Got to nip out, Wendy. Won't be long. Majollica's on her way over.

—What's happening, Lee? Have they found him?

—No.

—He's in the park. Where they're digging for the kiddies' playground. In the park.

I pecked the old dear on the hot cheek.

—See you soon.

—Touching, said the copper as I stepped out. Over here. He put a hand on my shoulder and lowered me into the back of the three-door panda. Wait there. Don't fiddle with the radios. I waited there.

Majollica passed the car and threw me a look that could have been sympathy in another lifetime. She disappeared down the slimy slope to where Wendy was barking on about Frank in the park.

It was dirty dusk when we got to the rear grille of the Chivermouth constabulary building. The WPC got out of the driving seat and went on ahead to make herself ready. The copper pulled me out by the arm.

—Friendly, I said and he squeezed tighter. I went through

into the maze that was law and order in our city. I was booked in.

—Lee Treble Cock, the reception bird smirked into her thick-knit V-neck policewoman's jumper. I knew it all anyway. It was the same if you were reporting a crime. It was the same if you were protecting the good people of Chivermouth and bringing down the record crime rate with your vigilance.

The copper put me in a small room with a shiny top table, a thin disposable ashtray full of butts and a long flat tape recorder. There was room for the table but they hadn't bargained on people. I pulled a metal chair out and contorted around to get on to the bright green cloth pad. I wrenched back in towards the table until my guts were held clamped. I rolled a fag and flicked into a ribbed plastic cup half-full of cold tea. The WPC came in and contorted into her chair and the copper got into his. We were all three up against the wall and there was a shiny table between us.

—You've seen one of these before? The copper labelled and slid a cassette into the recorder.

—Yeah. On the TV.

—It'll be on the whole time.

—Except for when I fall down the stairs.

The copper switched the recorder off.

—Except for when you break your knees all alone in your cell, he said. He switched the recorder back on with a warning face.

—DC Marcus Serpell and WPC Marina Sprott interviewing Lee Trebilcock on Sunday March 10. Time 6.44 p.m.

DC Serpell paused.

—Lee Trebilcock, I am questioning you about an incident that happened on Sunday March 3rd 1996 outside The King's Limb public house between the hours of seven and eight p.m.

—Last Sunday.

—That's correct.

—Well, go on then, I yawned.

—Would you like to start by telling WPC Sprott and myself what you were doing on the date stated?

—I can state that on the date stated I was having a quiet beer with my Uncle Septor Trebilcock in The King's Limb alehouse and that as far as I know that's not a crime in this country. Any coffee? I asked looking round.

—What time did you enter the premises, Mr Trebilcock?

—Dunno. Maybe seven or so.

—Do you recall any of the clientele in The King's Limb on that occasion?

—Do I recall them?

—Do you remember who was in there at the time?

—No. No idea at all. I was having a beer at the back with my Uncle Septor and his old mates.

—Do you recall a group of young people, students at the university, having a glass of beer, having a look through their books of study?

—No. The place was heaving.

—Do you recall seeing a group of two young women and two young men in outdoor clothing with books open seated to the left of the bar?

—No. I don't.

—Were you acquainted with any of the young people in this group?

—What people?

—Did you approach one of the students in this group?

—No.

The copper slid over a holiday snap of a dark-haired kid in a fleecy jacket near a rock pool.

—Did you approach this student?

—Never seen him before.

—Didn't you approach this student and ask him to go outside with you?

—May have done.

—Do you remember what you said?

—No.

The copper looked down at notes in a clip-close pocket notebook.

—Wasn't it: 'Come outside I've got something to tell you?'

—No.

—Didn't you tell him it was in his best interests to do so?

—No.

—Well, that's funny. Because the young women in this group recall a young man answering your description asking their friend to step outside for, he looked down at the notes, 'a sec'. Now perhaps you could shed some light on that for me?

—No, I couldn't. They're wrong.

—So you wouldn't mind getting in a line-up situation to sort that out then?

—I want a lawyer.

—Did you go with this young man into the back passage of The King's Limb on the evening of Sunday March 3rd?

—I want a lawyer.

—Did you leave this young man waiting in the back passage for your Uncle Septor Trebilcock to go outside and see to him?

—Eh?

—Did you return to the bar of The King's Limb while your Uncle Septor Trebilcock went out into the back passage?

—No I fucking didn't.

—Did you tell your Uncle Septor that the young man was in the back passage waiting for him?

—No! I don't know what you're on about!

—Didn't your Uncle Septor Trebilcock go out into the back passage and see to the young man?

—What do you mean 'see' to him?

—Do you have any objection to providing hair, blood and semen samples for elimination purposes?

—Semen? What the fuck is this? Are you saying—

—We're not saying anything. We've got a young man in a hospital bed with extensive wounds to the head, body and genitals and there are signs of sexual interference. Now if you've got an objection to my taking semen from you then we can proceed from there. I warn you now that failure to do so may prejudice your defence at a later date. The courts won't look kindly.

—What courts? What are you saying about my Uncle Septor?

—We'll be talking to your Uncle Septor directly.

—Are you getting any semen out of him?

—It's you we're concentrating on for now. I'll get you a jar and you can go in a cell. Look on the bright side. You want to be performing at a time like this.

—Fucking hell. I put my head in my hands. Someone had got up the student's trouser leg and they wanted a bottle of my semen. I didn't feel like I could get a boner if I was smothered all over in blonde birds' 44DD cup tits. The WPC cleared her throat.

10. Chivermouth Constabulary

The cell was spacious like I needed room for a full-length billiard table and maxi bar when all my future rested on was the speed of a wrist action. The copper left the door talk-flap open and I shouted after him.

—Close the fucking flap. It's personal in here.

—No-one's listening.

—Perverts, I muttered and unbuttoned my jeans to Union flag pants. My dick was as soft as the softest limp dick I'd known and it was curled up like a field mouse against my thigh.

—Oh fuck.

I took it up and started to wank. I squeezed my dick in my fist and worked it backwards and forwards from the base. I licked my fingers and spread them over my testicles. I held one thigh with one hand pushing against the other with my fingers to hold it away against the jean. I coated with spit from my palm.

I looked at the walls and tried to think arse shapes into the scratch marks and chipped paint. The bed ledge was shiny stone with a thin foam mattress. There was a crapper round a stone curtain and just as much space as you could need.

I knew the thin shiny pages of the home shopping catalogue photographically – when to flick forward, when to lick my forefinger and go back two or three. I knew the pictures and the words like any other kid that's turned to his own hand for the love the birds couldn't provide.

I fixed my face on the stone curtain and my mind on bikini briefs and I travelled my stationary eyes down to cotton mounds where I knew the skin split into two. I thought of the blackline picture boxes for granny figure shapers and square-inch body trunks showing off cotton gusset nylon teasers, waist size eight to eighty. I switched to high-waister slips in blue or pink flowers and roved my mind over petite muscly arses. I tried vests and flat chests and bud tits breaking out and I increased speed with trainer bras where the same tits pushed together in underwires and the nipples were squashed up to the school shirt V-neck line.

I pulled at my dick.

I pictured the electric hand tools, stopping at my favourite Bosch rechargeable all-purpose. I knew the page layout – matt green body and black on-off switch, drill bits laid out in increasing size starting with four-sixteenths centimetre going to one and a half inch dull that was touchable, so touchable you wanted to caress it, carved like a seashell by an expert robot. If you'd held it to your ear you'd get sea. If you held it in your hand you'd get semen. I ran down to sandpaper attachments that were revolving paddles of glass paper for difficult areas that you could insert into the body. The drill body. My mind was wandering.

I yanked on my dick.

The bird was in the bookshop stacking away the books with a lift and bend action but here was the blond bloke looking for that heavy reference title that no-one could find and the bird was turning her head and wetting her Scandinavian lips. The blond bloke was making book sizes with his hand. Up the stepladder and over the blond bloke's face and I was under her cling-film cunt looking up at the way it squeezed reaching for that heavy book. The book was down and the bird and bloke were in the fairy tale cuckoo clock town making their way to the randy mate.

—All right in there?

It was Serpell with a mouthful of canteen food.

—Fuck off, I turned away.

I slapped my dick.

Lorraine was on her hands and knees round the multi-glue with a lost contact lens and I was behind her with a method of contact that was all my own and she was starting in surprise with Claire loosening the neck edge of her floral blouson.

I leant over and tried to suck my dick.

Deborah was in a handkerchief bikini round a poolside, smearing coconut oil over her forearms. She couldn't stretch round to even her hips. She sat up with her legs open trying to turn round and reach her back. She didn't know I was there. I was on my hands and knees at her back, pouring oil on to my hands, coating her flesh with grease, slipping off the rolls, catching in the crevices, moving downwards to the sunken cloth line buried in her arse. I had my hands over her shoulders and across her back and around her waist and around her neck. Deborah was arching her inflatable back. I rubbed up and down and the skin shook and moved with a second's interval. I slapped at the fat that was thick and bright yellow under the white skin. I moved nearer to her arse, I slipped my hands round her waist, I wriggled to her crotch, I opened my legs around her back, I rubbed my dick against her, I whispered in her ear, I rode her back, I came into the wide-rim plastic jar.

I sighed without a sound. The duty nurse wanted a tube of blood and to pick off three strands of my hair with her tweezers. I ate a jellied beef hotpot from a plastic plate with cubicles for vegetables and mashed potato.

DC Marcus Serpell was a big man restrained by a shiny table into black and white check trousers. His face was big and his skin was thick and cream-coloured. His hair was short, curly and dark brown so as to be black. His eyes were small and active, his nose squashy and pitted like grapefruit skin. He had nostril and ear hair and you could see the texture of the chest hair under the thin white short-sleeve shirt. His arms were woolly with starter homo-sapien hair.

—Ever been to the Club Climax?

The recorder was back on and we were starting where we left off.

—For the benefit of the tape, Mr Trebilcock is shaking his head.

—For the benefit of the tape, Mr Trebilcock is here under false fucking pretences.

—It's a straightforward question.

—The Climax is for queers.

—And you're not queer.

—No.

—But you've got mates that are.

—I never said that.

—You've been in to see us before haven't you, Mr

Trebilcock? Shoplifting, incite to violence dropped on insufficient grounds, terrace hooliganism, urinating on the crocus beds. You're known to us. You've been cautioned on at least one drunk and disorderly. Your uncle has served time for child pornography possession and aggravated bodily harm.

—That's bollocks!

—He didn't tell you because you're his nephew.

—I'm not his nephew. He's my uncle.

—My mistake.

—You're telling me this kid was shunted up the arse and you think I had something to do with it!

—Which kid is that?

—You think I rogered that kid in the back passage.

—We don't think anything.

—That's about right.

—It's our job to get the facts.

—My Uncle Septor's not a poof. He's got a live-in housekeeper. Alison. Ask her.

—Oh, we'll be talking to Miss Lunch. What age was it you started having girlfriends, Mr Trebilcock? Late starter, were you?

—Thirteen. Sherry from Berwick-on-Tweed. Torquay hotel car park. You can check up if you can find her.

—Ever had leanings the *other* way?

—No. Have you?

—I'm not a suspect in a rape and assault case.

—Nor am I.

—Let's talk about the young man. He's got a name so we may as well use it. Michael McCarthy. Let's talk about Michael McCarthy.

—Who's that.

—That's the young man you approached last Sunday evening in the bar of The King's Limb. The young man you assaulted in the back passage. The young man who was in intensive care for three days and on his front in our rape suite when he should have been studying for his mock exams.

—I don't know any Michael McCarthy.

—Ever *done* it before?

—Done what?

—Prised a tight little backside open. Got a hard one. Given a rub down.

—You're a fucking pervert.

—Ever wanted to?

—What is this?

The WPC looked at Serpell's hot, red face. Serpell breathed in and out deeply and fiddled with the hound's-tooth check trousers under the cramped table.

—Take a break, said Serpell.

—Don't worry, WPC Marina Sprott said over the table. He's just in a bad mood. Did you manage your semen all right?

—Yeah.

—I nearly popped in.

—Oh.

—We're going to need you for a line-up tomorrow morning. Is that convenient?

—No. You'll have to charge me.

—Won't take long and it's only one night inside. Is it the first time?

—No.

—That's all right then. Urinating on the crocuses! I don't know. I'll get you some tea.

—I didn't do it.

—I can see you're a heterosexual.

—Get the tea.

Serpell came back in the sardine interview room and faced me across the table. He said they were working through my samples and I would have to wait until morning. I said I wanted to know what happened in the back passage that night and he said the kid was raped while he was lying unconscious along the base of the wall. He said he was dragged into the crapper for the act. I said I didn't do it. I felt sick like I would be sick. Serpell put me back in the cell. I picked up a blanket from storage on the way through. One pillow Serpell said as I lunged for three. He took my shoe laces and slapped the talk-flap closed.

I could sleep anywhere, on a train, on a plane, in an automobile. I could sleep in a cell. It wasn't so cold. But I couldn't sleep in that cell. So this was what it was like to be trapped. You had to keep calm. If you panicked you went over. If you screamed you didn't stop. I'd been in there half an hour. I was a nervy kid in tight places where it looked like the sight of daylight alone would make it worth while getting up in the morning. It was Chivermouth on Sunday night and it was quiet. It wasn't the Bronx. It wasn't crack addicts and rappers' gang warfare. It was drinking and driving outside Disco Glory and a tramp who couldn't remember his way home because he'd been homeless all his adult life. The doors swung open quietly and the men lay down and put their heads on the flat pillows and enjoyed the peace and quiet away from their wives, their mothers and the cold.

The plain walls were painted with heavy-duty paint that shone in the mute light. There were lines of half-hearted graffiti – ROB 19.2.93; WPC SPROTT FUCKS CHIMPS – but I didn't pay it the attention. You couldn't see it unless you got up close. I took a piss behind the stone curtain and walked about in my space. There was nothing to stop me. The cell was tall, the ceiling over fifteen feet above my head. There was a high window made up of small squares of dimpled glass so you couldn't see through. I could walk a circle of some paces before retracing. You didn't want to touch the walls. They weren't dirty but they looked like they could freeze a human fluid for eternity. I sat down on the end of the stone ledge and brought one leg up to my chest in the style of the old Hollywood stir-movie heroes. I was Jimmy Cagney wrongly imprisoned on chain gang row. I was a fugitive from a one-parent family. I would break into song.

I put my head against the shiny cold wall where all the heads of all the murderers had lain before me. I played the hero. Steve McQueen, the cooler king, the great escapist on Christmas afternoon when you couldn't give a fuck who was locked in any prisoner of war camp or who was digging little tunnels to get out and blown up on enemy lines. That's where it all started. All boys together. Any Tom Dick or Harry. Any dick after a busy day tunnelling under the huts squeezed into a gymnastic horse. I knew all about history. It wasn't sex. It was fear. Fear that you didn't have any respect. Fear that you liked Carruthers more than just holding hands after lights out. Holding together in the face of danger and wanting to hold together after too. I'd been a fucking boy scout until they wanted me to clean windows on Saturday morning for no money.

I slid down the wall and opened my mouth ready for sleep. The lights were on. The Daffy Duck curtains were in the police launderette. WPC Sprott had knocked off and I wasn't a chimp.

I dreamt I was in a long commercial deep freeze under dirty brown water being dragged to the bottom by a skin diver with a balaclava and lockable chains. I was struggling. I could see the top but the skin diver had the chains around me and I was drinking in the water and swallowing the fish shit bits. I was pulling at the balaclava to see who was at the bottom of the deep freeze but I couldn't get the wool through the nose bridge of the panel goggles. I got to the top and held on to the side with my arms shouting for help to a couple of figures on a chaise longue but they were ignoring me and I slipped back under and the skin diver got hold of me again so I was drinking and trying to get free and I could see the figures picking their toenails.

If it was dawn there was no morning chorus to tell me so. The high window was waxed over with road and car-tyre dust. How many people had stooped against the constabulary wall to look in at me I thought from my boner-aware position of lying on my back. How many people were standing round in the electric-door foyer wringing their hands, fumbling through the displays of curled drink-drive car stickers, chewing on the edge of a clean Monday morning sheet wondering when they would get a chance to see my face again to say they were sorry.

I knew it was dawn because it got lighter. The corridor lights went off. The voices spoke low outside my talk-flap. The keys sounded like hammers in the lock. One of the voices laughed. One coughed and cleared its throat. I heard the hammers at the same level as my ears and knew it was my turn. The door opened and a man with half a head of hair walked in with a briefcase. The man's eyes were black-rimmed and his skin looked loose on his face. He was in green corduroy trousers and a jacket with elbow patches. He was in comfortable shoes. He put one leg on the mattress and hung his body over it to look down at me. He held his hands out under his face so he could look at his nails while he was talking. I stayed lying down, the Cherokee-design orange and turquoise blanket up around my chin.

—I'm your brief, said the man. My name's Neil.
—Oh.
—Neil Glenhusky.

—What?

I pulled the blanket back off me and sat up, going at the man's shin with the side of my hand like a karate expert. Get off, get off, I said until the man put his leg down on the floor.

—No problem, I hope. Duty solicitor. I'm here to help.

—I don't need it. Are you connected to, I coughed, Alun Glenhusky, disco reviewer?

—Good heavens! cried the man. Yes, I am. He's my brother.

—Oh Jesus fuck.

—Have I missed something?

—Alun Glenhusky the London poof?

—I don't think so. My brother's married to a lovely girl. They've got new twins. I expect you've read something ambiguous in the trade papers.

—No. None of that. My best friend Hawley's getting one up the arse from him.

—Good Lord. It must be someone different. That's quite shaken me up.

—Think what it's done to me.

—It's a bit early. I've got to get some coffee. Look, they're putting you in a line-up. They think you were there at the . . . King's . . . the . . . wherever it was. I'll be there. I'll see you shortly.

The man left the cell and I got under the blanket so I couldn't see anything except for a row of wild ginger-colour horses stitched into a turquoise blue background. I didn't hear WPC Marina Sprott come in and it was a shock to get her hand on my abdomen in that way.

—Come on, Lee. We're ready for you now.

The WPC was close to me, squeezing my guts with her hand.

—It says you fuck chimps, I muffled through the blanket, keeping as still as I could.

—Don't worry.

—I'm tired. I gave too much semen yesterday. It's knocked me out. I could go home and come back later.

—We can't do that. The witnesses are ready. Your tests will be through soon.

—Don't you get any time off? You were here last night.

—Are you being cheeky?

—No.

—I thought you might be asking when my night off was.

—No.

—Oh.

WPC Marina Sprott clenched the spare skin that protected my intestines from the daily dust and she let me get up on my own. She watched as I undid my belt and let my jeans fall to my knees so that I held the material up by bending my thighs outwards. She didn't turn her head as I tucked my vest into my pants. She took my arm and guided me through the buff corridors, stepping aside for the plain-clothes boys to swing past looking for clues along the lino.

The line-up room was as roomy as the question room had been only someone had taken out the shiny table. There was a blank wall opposite a one-way gold mirror that sloped at an angle into a window frame. There was a shelf with plastic cups and sticks of chalk. There were plastic bibs with black numbers on.

Neil Glenhusky appeared.

—They just want you to stand around for a while, he said. Don't worry.

Serpell was on the heels of Glenhusky, pulling a plastic bib over his head, placing number three across his short-sleeve shirt.

—We're short on men, Serpell said.

I pulled on number five and hung around on one leg.

Other kids appeared. One was in a post office uniform. He was the postkid. Number seven was tall and skinny. WPC Marina Sprott got into number one. I said nothing. The room was small. I got elbowed by all the bodies getting bibs on.

—Get into a line in numerical order, Serpell told us and we straightened up and lumbered about until we worked out what number we were and what number everyone else was.

—One goes before two, Sprott.

It was early in the morning. Serpell stepped out and looked up and down the line at us. We stood up straight, turned to the left, spoke 'come outside for a sec' and leant our backs on the wall. I was called forward.

—Come outside for a sec, I told the gold mirror.

—It's all right. They're thinking about it, Serpell said. I accepted a light tar cigarette from the skinny kid and puffed thin grey smoke into the small room.

—You could be OK, Glenhusky said to me, biting his nailtips, turning his palms outwards. Serpell nipped outside. I didn't know what he was doing. Glenhusky hung around WPC Marina Sprott. The postkid shivered in the corner.

—Looks like it's positive for you, I whispered to the postkid as he squatted down using the right angle of the wall for support.

—I don't even know what it's for, the postkid whined with his head in his hands. I only came in for recorded delivery.

—Gang rape. Young bloke.

—Oh no. My mum'll kill me if they say it's me.

—Oh, it's definitely you all right. I can see through that thing.

I nodded at the gold mirror.

—Oh no, the kid whined.

Glenhusky approached as far as he could in the cramped room. Serpell pulled the bib off his head. We formed a triangle. The identification was positive. My semen was clear. They wanted me back tomorrow.

11. Poem for the Modern Man

I stepped into the constabulary reception like a goldfish slipping into a beaker after it's fallen out of its bowl. I couldn't turn around or see anything but I wasn't being flushed down the crapper.

A WPC in a flat hat looked me over from the bullet-proof glass. She wasn't getting any. The electric doors were tied open with string. The weapons amnesty bin was on the veranda. I cocked one leg and hopped over. I stood still and slowly rolled a fag on the slippery concrete. It had been raining. It was wet. Chivermouth was wet and used like the Matey Ones in St Dean's Cross roundabout church shell where the open-air lovers fucked to the rhythm of the bypass traffic under a fogged-up moon.

A kid pushed past me using his blown-out chest. I balanced roughly and looked behind at thick tousled hair, facial sideboards and a strong, veiny neck. The kid stopped at Neil Glenhusky in the foyer and stood around looking at Glenhusky's files until a copper came through the combination-lock door and signalled with one waving finger for them to go into the buff corridor. Glenhusky saw me as he was nudging the kid inside. He put his thumb up and I turned back to two flights of slippery steps looking down the slope to St Dean's Cross roundabout.

St Dean's Cross roundabout was named after St Dean, patron saint of the holy boy racer. The island was made of a church that had had a roof in a better time. Now it was hollow like a beetle body that's eaten from the inside. St Dean's was the type of roundabout where you got caught behind a full-length racing yacht on tow coming at you without brakes. It was the Chivermouth decider. Stay or go. Bypass or pedestrianized shopping centre. There were no rules. You pulled out when you wanted and slid across the lanes for wherever you were going or you came up in the bus lane looking testy like you had a handy sheath knife in the glove compartment. The church may once have been for those people in history that liked to get down on their knees in the name of something but now it was the sacred temple of Chivermouth where the birds got down on their hands and knees and took it so hard in the bowels they retched gin and orange on to the concrete. Students got over the road on to the roundabout in summer with bottles of Mexican lager and coloured barbecue torches that stuck in the ground and fell over when the wax was burnt. The constables knocked off the early graveyard shift and sent them home or shouted at them when they couldn't get through the three-deep traffic.

.The church was held together by steel poles so the walls didn't fall apart on the cars below. There wasn't much to see inside except half-full Matey Ones joined together at the rims with semen glue, lying about like fallen blossom on the floor. There were beer cans squeezed together at the middle and burger van serviettes puckered with ketchup where the birds' lips wiped. There were pale brown fag butts showing tips that had drawn off golden nicotine to the end of the white paper.

There were twenty-two steps but I took them in eleven, hunching over the wet rusty handrail. I touched the pavement and took the subway, popping up on the other side of the road like a day-vision mole. It was one of those Monday mornings where you're disappointed the cigarship spacemen didn't get you on board for permanent questioning. It was Chivermouth like you knew it. Sky like a lid on a biscuit tin, sun in overcast coverlets wanking over the early morning Unity Street lovers, clouds blazing a trail of 'why the fuck did I bother'. Roads rain-slicked to old-age pensioner danger, pavements making facial reflections out of footprints that lasted a second, bus queues locked together by the chance the next red shape would be the one.

Boy babies in crew cuts slumped against tits on buses looking dead, toddlers stamped in toddler coats dreaming of kid coats, kids burnt fag holes in kid coats dreaming of sheepskin-lined men coats, men in sheepskin-lined coats dreamt of shrouds and earthen coats.

All the city buildings in Chivermouth nearly touched so you could throw a stone between them if you had one big enough or the time and inclination to spare. The university was on the next roundabout. I could read. I'd seen the sign on the building wall before it fell into the canteen through cowboy workmanship. UNIVERSITY OF CHIVER-MOUTH it had read in a circle of tables on the local news.

The university was a ten-floor building. It had a ground-floor library with a glass top made into a pyramid. There was a canteen around the entrance and parking space if you belonged or you had a fleecy jacket and a family that lived three hundred miles away so you got your washing sent through the post. There were no classrooms. Just old men in elbow-patch corduroy jackets steering fibreglass cars round cycle paths and fat cooks in white overalls sitting on stools outside kitchens puffing fags.

I'd been on campus. I'd had a boxed batch of Bunsen burners away for the dragon-chasers and I'd had slippery rucksacks from the library basement where the fleecy jackets had their noses up against the computer screens waiting for the magic to begin. I'd been up in the lifts of Roald Amundsen Building and stalked the sloping rooms with the swing-top desks and I'd seen the wallcharts of bionic limbs and walking robots that went into volcanoes on scouting expeditions. I'd poked my head through the doors of the grey-haired men wiring radios together and the old birds typing from yellow paper files. I'd ridden a fucking potter's wheel with clay hands holding on to a kid's exam jugs to get close to a blonde bit in a fleecy skirt. I'd eaten subsidized roast beef, parsnips and gravy off a white glass plate grinding on spilt salt grains at a canteen table with a media workshop of eager birds videoing my mastication. I'd simulated sex with groin rubbing up against the leaded pyramid with a French bird at a student entertainment event where a northern kid dressed as a girl and threw paste pearls into the crowd of six or so desperate twats. I knew what campus life was. Ten floors of prefab over a library dug half into the ground and Barbican hostels built with taxpayers' money to make the steel gangplank stairways and security locks that changed once a month. I'd forced my way through the surfhappy kids blocking up the subway with their vinyl sausage bags of underpants and tracksuit bottoms. And I'd nutted the pissed twat that put his hand in my face when I was ordering a lager top in JFK's Hot Conspiracy Disco Club.

The library doors were in a line for entering and exiting. There was no security lock. The public could get in there if they wanted to hang around with the pimply birds in cardigans and dry-haired Europeans asking you where the books were. I pushed on an ENTRY door and pulled an EXIT bar towards me. A library bird shouted after me and I slipped down into photocopying for the urinals.

The urinals were next to the head librarian's office. The head librarian was a fat bird. The fat bird was in her office. She looked up. Maybe my overnight shirt was giving it away. Too clean for the student life of no washing powder. I took a clean white bowl and unzipped. I aimed my dick at the ceramic and leant back closing my eyes. I pushed out with my abdomen. I frothed up and got the smell sharply in my nose that told me I was processing correctly my daily liquid intake. I shook and replaced, splattering my pants. I zipped up and yawned.

There was a kid next to me looking at the wall. The kid's hair was in the start of whiteman's dreadlocks and he was in an unwashed weekend surf sweatshirt.

The kid was the type of kid to call you 'man' and use the word 'maximum'. I smoothed my jean crutch and looked at the wall.

—Know where the jewellery depot is, mate? I asked in a pleasant manner.

—What's that? The kid gave me a friendly student look that would get his brains bashed out in a better place.

—Er, the jewellery depot. My bird's studying how to make jewellery. Necklaces and that, you know. Jewellery.

—Your bird? Oh, right. There's a map in the main building foyer. I'm Bionic myself.

—Bet you fucking are. I said 'ta' and made the exit.

The main building floor was made of scarlet lino and there were noticeboards round the walls with rooms to let, bird typists to type your essay and insurers to insure your mountain bike against paint chip. The map was in a foreign language. I asked the receptionist bird in the cubicle.

—What floor's jewellery, love?

—That'll be fifth.

The bird fancied me.

I pressed for the wind-up Otis lift that was going to get me a few feet nearer to heaven. I gangled with a pair of Chink birds nattering in their language about who they were shagging. I rubbed against the rucksack of Yoko Ono to get her in the lift quickly and we rode in silence until I forced out at five.

I'd been in the corridors before. The walls could have been cell walls but the students didn't streak their walls with shit or else someone cleaned up afterwards.

You knew what room was what because you looked through the vertical letter-box fibreglass window that was above the door handle. The letter-box window was there to stop the old men teachers touching up the birds in lessons. The inspectors could walk round checking up on the old ones and the bird students could lodge complaints. I walked down the corridor and looked through. I recognized the pottery room and the gifted ones pulling on lumps of clay that were finished works of art and the photography labs where the birds were dressed in black with purple hair, holding up strips of negatives to the window because their fucking pictures were so fucking weird they didn't know which way up they went after they got them back from the chemist.

I smelled the perfume of one thousand rotting roses and sensed in my nose that I wasn't too far from jewellery. It was at the end of the corridor in a bay with metal and material chairs. The door was written with SILVER AND GOLD-WORK FASHION ACCESSORY STUDY ROOM. I worked it out for myself. There were dimpled pictures of wrists, necks and ears on the walls. I passed a finger ring bigger than my head. I could have conversed with a studded nose. I chose to sit down on one of the chairs. I rolled and lit up a fag putting one ankle up on to one leg. I sunk my head into my neck so my chin was balanced on the neck edge of my Emporio Georgina sale shirt. Kids in twos and threes passed me and singled out to get past my foot that was level with their hips. They looked at me like I wasn't in their club and I wasn't.

I hadn't been invited to wear a fleecy jacket or jeans that were rubbed away at the crotch through self-handling. I hadn't been invited to measure the shopping centre rainfall in a plastic cup or work on clay lumps for graduate exhibition. I'd been left off the list to talk bollocks over cider and blackcurrant in the student bar with a bunch of others that looked just like me. I'd been too busy trying to get a life so I could buy Wendy's council home and find a blonde bird to breed with and buy a car with a 'Z' and 'X' in the nameplate. I'd been on the do-it-yourself list to wear a romper and direct clientele to the wallpaper paste and the putty and the paper shade charts and the self-tapping screws and the garden fork and hoe sets.

I finished the fag and put it out on the sole of my shoe. There was a window at the end of the corridor that didn't open. I tried. It didn't open. I put my face up and looked down at the pyramid and building tops where trash was dumped in thin plastic body sacks. I could see the grass of the paths that was scratched off by the bright yellow bicycles. I could see the kids huddling up for protection against the student union sweetshop and the do-it-yourself launderette. I watched them slip on the wet concrete slabs outside the library and grab each other's sleeves to hold them upright. It was an exclusive club. It excluded me. And I'd put one of their number into intensive care on my night off. Ha ha. Ha.

I put both hands in my jacket pockets so I was hugging my waist. I pushed through the door in daytime darkness so that my eyes shrank on the other side where the light was coming from.

The jewellery room was like the pottery room except there were no claydust handprints or drying busts or little china turrets for balancing goblets in the kiln so they didn't touch each other. I knew all about pottery. I'd glazed and fired the kid's exam jugs in primrose slip. There were long tables with shiny tops and room to get your legs in underneath if you sat on a stool. There were trays of stones and beads like dried peas or beans. There were glue-joined Do It Easy boards covered in blue and black velvet pinned with rock necklaces and earrings and rings. There were scarves wound around noticeboards for inspiration. I noted a couple of African tribeswomen posters with dusky birds holding multi-pierced nostrils.

Deborah said she didn't know if things happened for a reason. I knew they did. I didn't have to holler words of love hoping that Deborah was packed into the pyramid of study along with the fleecy ones because she was right there against the sky, like a papier mâché volcano on a newspaper island, like a folded lilo on a dry-ice rink, like a Michelin man on an auto rescue pick-up truck.

Deborah was at the end of the room with her back to me on a small blue settee working her hands over her lap. She was shimmering against the fifth-floor sky. Of all the university rooms on all the floors on all the campus she had to be sitting in this one. I was looking at her. She was humming to herself, a tune made famous by a cult lanky American twat who'd overdosed on life and blown it with a Beretta in a hotel room leaving a suicidal two-year-old and a tart for a wife. Her hair was clean and I could see her shoulders, round and drooping on to her sides as she sat working. I went closer to her neck and looked at her head bent over. Her neck went into her back and into a wideneck blouson. I could see the start of her mountain-range spine. I could see the little hairs. Her neck was smooth and white like the sand in the Majorca holiday brochures. Her hair was limp on her skull. I could see her pink skin scalp.

I stood behind and watched her arms troubling to come together across her wide waist. Her feet were set apart to let the thighs sit comfortably. There was a radio but the only noise was the kill-me-quick lyrics of the dead man on the pursing lips of the fat girl. I leant up against the back of the low sofa.

I cleared my throat.

—On the side, said Deborah looking ahead of her at the window on to the sky. Little plug socket fuses. They look ever so good with the amethyst. Adrian's drilled holes in them with his special crafts drill.

Deborah was talking to no-one and I was that no-one.

Quickly I turned and pulled up a low crafts stool from under the long table. Deborah looked down again. I yanked a tray of glass beads towards me and started some artwork of my own. I pushed papers out of the way to get my space and worked quickly joining up the beads into simple writing. A kid pushed through the door in a tiara of horseshoe nails and a chain-mail mini-dress. I ducked low and worked on. I stuck my tongue out of one side of my mouth to help me concentrate.

The kid in the tiara barked at Deborah on the settee.

—All right, Debs?

I worked quickly selecting my material to complete my project. No-one came and no-one saw. I pulled the final strands of the piece together and made for the door. I found the lift, skulked round the stairwell then pitched forward and took the stairs by three until I made ground. I breathed in and out fast as I pushed my way through the birds and blokes hanging on the wall outside the study pyramid.

—Oi, 'scuse me, said the students after me but I was gone to the hopper bay where the little bus was waiting for me like it knew I needed it more than any other day.

I monkey-walked along the stainless steel stabilizer bars to the back of the bus and swung into a raised platform two-seater ahead of a pair of day-tripping old dears. The old dears were exchanging the regular comments that stopped them from dropping off and I didn't stop them. I turned to the window. I felt a sudden pain in my digestive system as I saw that old people were the same as me but with different experiences and shrivelled-up skin. So they talked to stop themselves from dying. And I thought they liked it.

The barbecue set was on the forecourt when I crossed the roundabout. That was Morgan being keen. You could trust Morgan.

I crossed the corrugated threshold and slipped up through plastic storage into wood and otherwise manufactured shelving. I heard Ronald's comfortable shoes on the floor before I saw him and when he came around the aisle corner I quickly shot up into the Gents to get into the spare romper I kept in my lock-up.

I joined Ronald behind the plastic curtain.

—Keep an eye on the clock, young Lee, Ronald said quietly with a glance that said more than the words. Ronald could have been a vicar if he'd had a belief in God and hadn't needed the cash from supervising.

—Sorry, Ronald. Got held up. Won't happen again. I see Morgan beat me with the show barbie this morning.

—Yes, that's right. And Lorraine's sick in the canteen. She's under the weather. I've left her with a regional branch line glossy to thumb through. It's nice for the pictures if she doesn't want to bother with the words.

I looked at Ronald.

—Yeah, OK.

—It's only fair of me to tell you, Ronald's face looked grave. Lorraine's been in to have a word with Pete. She says that you've been bothering her.

I was hot in my twenty-six-hour furry chin growth. I changed from one leg to another in the baggy romper.

—She's confused.

I thrust Ronald a manly look.

—She says there was some friction in Morning Tuscany and that you've been giving her trouble.

—She's lying then! She's having her *time of the month*, I explained. She told me. That's what happens. They imagine things and cry a lot. I've seen it before.

—Well, that's what she says. I've not known Lorraine to imagine things. We all noticed you were keen on her.

—What's she been saying?

—I'll have to leave that to Pete. He's got enough on his plate with the rechargeable oscillating fans. They won't switch off. I've put them outside for the meantime.

The oscillating fans had been on the go since Friday morning.

—OK, Ronald.

I skipped down to customer services.

Morgan lifted his eyes on my approach. He put them down

again. I nodded my head. He turned to make conversation with a tall kid with a fine chestnut ponytail purchasing a roll of lining paper. I edged up to the counter and made a play for the carriers to pack the plain paper roll but Morgan had his hand over the dispenser before I got there. I looked at him and he looked away.

—Nice day, Morgan, I said. Claire was at his side, holding his arm like he couldn't do the transaction on his own.

—Lorraine's up in the staff canteen, said Claire, firing tiny missiles across the wide mouth of her estuary. She sounded desperate and authoritative. She squeezed Morgan's arm. Morgan held her hand and thanked the kid with the chestnut ponytail.

—Ta, Claire, love, I said and left the cosy-booth twosome.

It was quiet in the staff area. I peeped through into the canteen and got a look at Lorraine on a grey plastic chair scratching her thigh top with her fingernail. I could hear the rasping noise. It was that kind of a scratch. I pushed on the door with my shoulder and Lorraine's hand jumped back to her lap. She looked up and then away.

Lorraine Gets An Apology

—Got the phone message, I said and stood there. That was Majollica. Not my old dear. Majollica lives over the road.

Lorraine looked down at a red broken nail that looked like it would catch and pull threads on any item of clothing. She wasn't on the ledge with the microwave. She was at the round plastic table I used for my lunch box.

—What's all this about, then?

Lorraine began to cry.

—It's you, she said, without lifting her knuckles to her sockets to stop the tears.

—What about me?

—You know. Getting me in that cupboard while the shop was still open. Leaving me there with my pants' label stuck in the sink-pipe join. Anyone could have seen. It was demeaning.

—What d'you mean, 'demeaning'?

—Making me do that to you like that.

—I didn't know your panties got stuck.

—They did.

—You enjoyed it.

—You're such a . . . man.

—That's what you like. You're a randy girl.

—You took advantage of me. You put me under the sink while you chattered away with Claire. Being clever.

—You're overwrought with your Ray. That's what it'll be.

—No. You're making me say it exactly otherwise you won't admit it. That's what you do.

—You don't even know what you're talking about.

—I've seen Pete.

—I hope you'll be happy together.

—I've seen him about the harassment.

—Who's going to believe you? You're a known randy cow.

—It's the truth.

—You wanted it. If I got my dick out now and waved it in front of you you'd snap it up like a hungry croc.

Lorraine put her hands up to her head sides so they were like barn doors and she could only see straight in front of her.

—No. I just wanted to be looked after. I wanted someone to care about.

—That's what we all want.

—If it wasn't for Ronald and his wife I'd have left working here and Ray would have had to cancel his ski lessons.

I sat down with Lorraine at the table and pushed tartlet crumbs around with my thumb flesh.

—Well, that would have been a shame. How is your Ray?

—OK. He's coming home soon, she sniffed.

—You're in a fucking state, aren't you?

—Why did you chase me around the kitchens all of that time and act as if you fancied me?

—Dunno. S'the way I am. Can't help it. I'm a man.

—No, you're not. A man knows how to treat a woman.

—Like your husband? You go looking for it, Lorraine.

—I thought you were better than that.

—Did you?

—Yes.

—Oh well. Now you know. I'm as bad as the next twat.

—You're not.

—Maybe.

I got up and walked over to the sink. I clawed the tea bags out of the drainer and ran the cold water tap until the water was clear. The sink was slicked with grey film from general use. I turned and leaned with my front to Lorraine.

—I thought we could have had something, she said.

—What like? She was a dog with a Bonio. A hand job in outdoor furniture? Unprotected soixante-neuf in bathroom fittings?

—I didn't know you spoke French.

—I don't.

—A relationship.

—No offence, Lorraine, but you shag strangers in cupboards at work.

—So do you.

—I'm a man.

—I'm a woman.

—Now you've lost me. Anyway I'm a committed man. I'm spoken for.

—A beautiful blonde teenage girl from the girls' school?

—Something like that. Look, I'm trying to understand what you're saying but it's going ahead of my requirements as a bloke.

She started crying again.

—You used me. You took me for what you wanted. You knew I liked you.

—Pull yourself together.

—You've ruined me.

—You've ruined yourself.

—I'm going ahead with the charge.

—You can't.

—I can.

—You agreed to get in the cupboard.

—They'll believe me.

—I'm starting a new life. I don't need this. I've met someone.

—You won't say you're sorry.

—No. I won't. I'm not sorry.

—You're a bastard.

—Probably. Didn't have a dad.

—That's what it's all about, isn't it? You didn't have a dad so everyone else has got to be hurt too.

—Eh?

—You're just passing it on.

—No.

—Ray doesn't have a dad. How do you think he feels?

—Dunno.

—He's got a disease. He jerks. He can't help it. How do you think that feels?

—I don't think. I'm a man.

—Supposing he wants to do things like you do? Supposing

he wants to have a job like you do? Or a girlfriend? How can he?

—Got to go, Lorraine.

—You don't care. You'll only care if I say it right. In your language. Then you'll treat me right. You don't care about me when I act like you do. You want me to be better than you are.

—Fuck me. You're a bit full of it today.

—I did fuck you.

—You've been watching the late-night lesbian shows with the university teachers.

—No. I worked it out for myself.

—Is that a fact?

—You say you're sorry to me, Lee Trebilcock, and I'll drop the case.

—You've changed, Lorraine. I don't know what I saw in you. You're nothing but a dirty lesbian.

—Say you're sorry.

—Oh, fuck.

—Say it.

—Jesus. What do you want from me – a word?

—No. You can mean it.

—Morgan and Claire aren't talking to me. This is my fucking career. Ronald thinks I'm trouble. Who d'you think you are?

—You're feeling compromised.

—You're a walking fucking textbook.

—That's what I felt like when you left me in that cupboard with my skirt up near my face.

—You like it that way.

—All you've got to do is say you're sorry.

—You think I'd listen to you?

—You won't do it again.

—You're saying you don't want it now?

—Not with you.

—You've got it bad.

—Everyone will know.

—You've gone too far now.

—Say you're sorry.

—Oh Jesus Christ.

—Say it.

—It's your time. Post-menstrual fucking aggression. You're all the same you birds.

—You say you're sorry to me.

—Sorry, I lunged into Lorraine's wet open face. OK? Off my case?

—Louder.

I was hearing things.

—You better kiss the cheeks of my hairy arse, Lorraine sweet!

We paused as if a third person had said something important.

—All right. I'm SORRY. Now get back into kitchens, will you? You'll have customers waiting.

I went and urinated so hard against the wall I caught the splashes around my mouth. I swore and wiped my mouth with the back of my hand. I went back down on to the floor looking straight ahead of me. I felt Morgan and Claire look up. I ignored them. Lorraine came out of the staff door. She didn't look like she'd been in the same conversation. She looked calm. She got back into kitchens and took up her standing position in Morning Tuscany. I put my head down and went through the plastic curtain to see what needed my attention.

On the fifth floor of Roald Amundsen Building, in the silver and goldwork fashion accessory study room, on a

Formica table bench of glass beads and horseshoe nails, there was a poem written in catgut and rhyme:

LEE LUVS DEBRA
4 EVER
2 GETHER
4 NEVER
2 PART.

12. Uncle Septor Goes Twenty Leagues

I knew Uncle Septor would be out of his house the moment I saw the trike on the road and the bulldog bitch leashed to the gutter.

—Emergency meeting! he shouted from the tunnel like it was Christmas, New Year and Easter. I crossed over the road and let my feet rest on someone's pavement kingdom. Everyone's pavement was their kingdom. It just worked that way. There wasn't much to go round.

—Hear me, Lee?

—Busy, I said, one leg triangular against the wallside, my trainer suckering on cement joins.

—No, you're not.

He waded to the edge of his grass wetting his trouser legs. I hoisted up on to the wall behind me and put one arm around a redbrick post that was hollow in the top for growing chin-level flowers. He put his hands on his hips and stood half-on half-off the grass. He was in slippers. He looked as if he'd left his last fag burning on the edge of a matchbox.

—Got to talk to you, I shouted from on the wall, from over the road, from another man's kingdom.

—What about?

—Police want to see you.

—That's no worry of yours.

—They say you did things to that kid.

Uncle Septor ran towards his little black gate and held on to the top like a kid that thinks he will never go further than his own front garden. I knew the Samurai sea warrior under his cardigan would be flexing up for open warfare with his shoulder blades.

—You keep your mouth shut!

—They say you've got to give them some semen. I rubbed my groin bossily. It was giving me an itch.

—Shut it, son. Here and now. Unless you want me over that road and give you a sharp backhander!

—Come on then.

—Get yourself over here now!

—No.

—You did all right last week.

—So?

—You're needed tonight. It's the fruity one. He's been up your trouser leg. He'll be all over the estate with his disease.

—That kid was interfered with.

—You'd better keep it down.

—Your Alison said you left the merchant navy with more than a sore throat.

—Alison's gone. I'm doing my own housework. Are you coming over or not?

I slid off the wall and in through the little black gate.

The bulldog bitch was dribbling in the tunnel.

There were no folding chairs. The television was in the corner on Alison's wooden wheelie trolley and the floral settee was at an angle across the wall that led to the kitchenette. The kitchenette beads were hooked over a painting of root vegetables against velvet. Reg was on the settee in front of a thin coffee table that curved upwards at both ends and stood on the carpet in little metal boots. Boys and men were ranged against the walls leaning or squatting, jackets zipped, buttoned or Velcroed to their chins. A pair of blond kids were looking like angels on the window sill pressing at the curtains with their fingers.

—Bertha's outside with tummy trouble, Uncle Septor whispered as I passed by. I got down into a squatting position by the electric fireside. I hadn't changed for thirty-five hours. My face was as rugged as the underarms of DC Marcus Serpell.

—We'll take two of you with your videos and two on stills so check your batteries now. Mick'll take the front door and get things started. Reg was giving his knuckles a massage on the sofa. He'll have white spirit with him so whatever you do, don't get too close. We can't afford to lose anything. We can't take everyone. Lee's Septor's boy. He's had the trouble. Otherwise you can see it next week in an extended session here. As normal.

The men moved around from one foot to the other.

—Remember – keep your heads down. Septor's had the constabulary round. Got to be on our toes. Mick, get Bertha out of the fucking tunnel. She's bringing up grass.

The boys moved off slowly.

I stood around and waited.

Uncle Septor went up the road. Reg stayed on the back patio, smoking Bullmaker's Golden, spitting at the garden furniture. He put his foot up on the white plastic chair and took it down again. He whirled the washing line with his forehead. He kicked the grass. I stayed inside and put my feet up on the floral settee.

—Your friend's going to cop it tonight, Reg shouted in from the patio.

—Yeah, I said and flicked through the satellite channels for Uncle Septor's pay-as-you-watch channel. It was nestling at Channel Fifteen but the meter was low and the figures were like quick-moving clouds. You could just hear groans. I took a look along Uncle Septor's lounge cabinet shelf of videos and specialist tricycling magazines. He had a couple of books bound in green vinyl. There were some old paper comics of men doing bodybuilder poses in leopardskin trunkettes. The pictures were old. There were adverts for exercises. The men had thin shins and elevated thighs. They stood about like women with their fists clenched like apes' around the hips and chests. You could be taller or a new man in seven days. The magazine was called *Physical Architecture* magazine. It was old. He had *Trike Enthusiast* and *Education Nature Trail* with the pictures of the schoolboys in shorts running along the seaside headlands among the gorse and birds' nests. It made me think of Hawley and the cut-out artworld penises he stuffed into his chest of drawers for easy reach. Uncle Septor had a thin body. Maybe he wanted to learn the exercises.

Uncle Septor's kitchenette had been left in a hurry by someone who would normally be clean. There was a used sheet of oven paper with the marks of hastily removed nests, and sink bowls stacked so each got to soak in water with the metal spoons in the smallest. There was no room in the kitchenette. If you'd tried swinging a gerbil you'd have had the RSPCA round. Uncle Septor had the place stacked with Chubby's wrappers and pizza boxes that said FRESH PIZZA on the side because Chubby didn't have a special name for the pizza side of the business and the boxes were cheap. I wasn't going to touch the empty cans that were covered with flaky grey ash. Maybe I'd put all the beer in one can and give it to Uncle Septor. Maybe I wouldn't. Reg was out through the kitchenette door on the scrub grass waiting for the moment when they would start the hare running and he could chase round after it until he got tired. I was waiting for a fish dinner.

Uncle Septor came back with three cones of chips jammed between his fingers and a thin carrier bag of fish wrapped in paper. I sat on the window sill and threw chips at my face with a two-prong chip fork. I pulled fish off skin and slipped that in too. Uncle Septor had beers open. I asked him about the magazines. He said he was holding them for a friend and not to ask if I wanted a quiet life. Reg sat over his chips like a fussy vulture. Uncle Septor drank a can and screwed his chips up into a paper ball which he threw into the kitchenette.

—Shame about your Alison, I said.

—Shut it, Uncle Septor said.

Reg switched to a nature channel and we watched the habits of a colony of manual-stimulation monkeys that wanked themselves off against each other all day even when they were related. The monkeys got up in the morning, passed each other on a tree bough, got their dicks out and slipped them over their little cousins and nephews and nieces and sons and daughters. Then they went down to the dining area and wanked against their sister or brother before breakfast. Then they walked around the jungle and wanked against tree boughs until it was time for bed and they found a quiet spot to calm down.

—Fucking animals, said Reg.

We watched a movie about a pickpocket who ran a tight team at public events in America. The pickpocket ran it like a police operation. It was slick. It was exciting. I wanted to go to America and be a pickpocket. It was a better living than the Do It Easy.

We watched the old man that cut up dead people to discover cause of death and it was always suspicious. The programme was from 1977. The man was a busy man named after a fruit. Maybe he was a fruit. The man went to give a lecture on bones at a college and one of the keener kids gave him a gift of a bone dug up on the campus building site. That's the way it was in that programme. Murder all around. The bone came from where the new canteen was going so the old man stopped the digging and didn't find any supporting ribs or skull but he built a murder mystery out of the one bone until he had a clear picture of the dead bloke and the dead bloke was a blond Scandinavian-origin league football player from Lubbock, Texas that was killed in 1958. After that it was easy. I was the only one watching. Reg was back on the patio with the Bullmaker's and Uncle Septor was washing-up at the sink in Alison's housework overall. Bertha had been back at the front door scratching but no-one had let her in.

Uncle Septor came in with a little tortoiseshell tea tray. I used the milk and wrung a tea bag over a cup. The water was cold. Uncle Septor crossed his legs on the settee so I saw the linings of his slippers. He wrapped his legs together tightly and took out his fag tin. The tin was in the palm of his hand as if it was on display and he dipped his long fingers in so they worked the tobacco like chopsticks. He squeezed a small ball of tobacco and let it wait in the tin. He put the tin down on the coffee table, licked the first finger of one hand and slipped a cigarette paper out of a small green book of a hundred or more. He held the paper open with one finger and thumb, put the tobacco ball in and pulled along. The paper edges levelled and one clipped inside the other to make a fine sausage. Uncle Septor lit and sucked. He put the tin on its lid on the table.

It was dark. Uncle Septor clicked the television off at the remote control. Uncle Septor's remote control played a tune if you whistled. That way you could find it quickly if it slipped down the back of the settee. I whistled and clicked the television back on at the set.

—You can be a big fanny when you want, said Uncle Septor.

Reg came in and walked round the settee quietly. We were getting jumpy. We were like arch-intelligent robbers that had been planning a bank job for two years and it was two hours to go.

—Get control of yourselves, growled Reg.

—It was him.

—Fucking wasn't.

—Doesn't matter who it was.

Bertha scratched on the door.

—Let the fucking dog in.

It was quarter to twelve. I felt like I'd been kidnapped by a couple of lazy terrorists.

—Do what I say, Uncle Septor said to me.

—Fucking won't,' I said.

Uncle Septor got out of his slippers and sat down on the edge of the settee to pull on the slip-on boots. Reg tied the leather belt of his sports jacket into a bow. I brought my arms forward and smelt the smell of my own stale sweat. It wasn't a bad smell. I held my rough chin with one hand as if I was sampling a tit. Uncle Septor's trouser material got caught in the elastic of his boot. He got into the donkey jacket.

—All be the same in a hundred years' time, said Uncle Septor.

—Give him hell, said Reg.

—I want to watch Fordyce of the Bush, I said.

—No you fucking don't, Reg said.

We left the house and found Bertha in a pool of her own bile. She got up and followed us up the road.

Hawley Gets A Visit

We were animals. We slept at night because we couldn't see where we were going or what we were doing. We closed our eyes when we couldn't see and we opened them when we could. When it got dark we let our minds have the thoughts we didn't allow in the light-time. We trusted we weren't going to come and tip each other off our mattresses. We lived close to the earth in tiny boxes so we never touched. We pressed down with our finger and we had light, we pressed up and we had dark. We thought we'd ruined the earth because we thought we were that fucking clever.

The road was quiet. The light was orange above us as if we were following a nearer sun. Uncle Septor and Reg covered the pavement. I stamped silently behind in rubber-sole trainers. I knew the route they would take down through the houses. There was a light in the passage that switched on when you stood under it. The light switched on and we slipped into the little lane that took us from one estate to the other. It was midnight. The lights were going off and the houses were closing down. The world was disappearing for twelve hours as we walked on to Hawley's.

Night-time was the time when nothing ever happened and everything always did. It was when the sexes fucked, the couples split and the kids bit into their bottom lips, the time when the Chivermouth constabulary called over with news of the motorcycling son found flat on the ring road with coach treads in his belly. I knew what time it was. It was the time when no-one was there to tell you it was going to be all right, the time the skin healed over and the gaps were made, the time when the old ones couldn't get past the kiddy safety sealer on their own medication. It was the time when the fairies at the end of the garden left a quid under your pillow and put the tooth on the tiles of the crapper window sill and the cats howled under your window so you could understand the language of the sounds and it was 'let me in'.

It was the kind of time when the world was a slap in the face but it was a slap in the face you could take. When the old birds cleaned under their chins with facial lotions at mirrors in bedrooms where they was only room for the bed and the old men stood in the garden puffing on a last fag, watching the cat dip its back to piss on the flower bed. It was the time when the old people rattled about on pink electric blankets and the babies farted liquid into nappies in cots lined with plastic baby aids.

It was as cold as Chivermouth got in March and that meant stamping faster. Uncle Septor was coughing and bending and I could see his smoke, the type of human smoke that came with the cold. Bertha's sides banged against my leg. I clipped her with my reinforced plastic toe and heard my rubber shoes slap on the pavement.

Uncle Septor and Reg were in the mouth of the passage like Victorians on early morning stroll. They were talking business. They were relaxed. They passed the lines of cardboard castles that faced each other. The castle drawbridges were up and the milk bottles were out. The daffodils hung their heads on to the floor, trodden in, dirty, finished. The grass slunk away like oil slicks on a turning tide. It wasn't real grass. It was to keep the worms underground while the people were still alive and the cars ticked like tin clocks.

Uncle Septor and Reg tiptoed through the miniature kingdom and the babies gagged on bad mothers' milk and the men waved paper flags and the women baked Arctic Roll in windy kitchens wearing half-crotch teddy suits from the mail-order pages of the newspaper with the nude birds in the football socks.

In the houses, the lights were little fires behind thin patterned curtains that never opened. I knew the types of lights – two-pronged wall-socket candelabra with twisted-flame bulbs, plastic lampshades in ceiling clusters hanging on gold-coloured chandelier stalks, apple-shade spotlights turned low at the wall dimmer, single bulbs burning like dead men in empty rooms, stiff Dralon bobbly lampshades swaying on easy tables when the aeroplanes went over so quietly no-one heard but the attic shook.

Hawley was in his room. I could see the light behind the blackberry curtains where the lava lamps played at being bottled oceans. Hawley had material curtains not nets. He said he liked the feel. I stood on the tarmac and looked up while Uncle Septor shouted in whispers and crouched in the shade.

—Get here!

I went over to the other side of the road and leant against the street lamp so my arms were folded and one leg wasn't being used. I looked up at the sky and drummed one set of fingers against my arm. I looked around. That was what you did if you weren't involved. If you were standing too close to a fat girl or a poof in a shop queue you looked at the ceiling and left too much room for them. It just caught them on the side of the head.

Mick and Stevie were on their way up the road with two

kids from the club. The kids were big, twenty or twenty-one, in boots, waist-length black leather jackets and grey jeans that rolled over the boot-tops. I could see they had little handheld video recorders in one hand. Stevie had the still camera over his shoulder and a tripod under one arm. Mick was pulling at the tripod from behind. Uncle Septor and Reg were bickering in the bushes.

—Got to get the light right, said Stevie.

I ran my tongue over my front teeth, looking away.

—Not using flash on this one. Natural light's good with flames. Fast film. Got to use the tripod. Keep it still. Know what I mean?

—Fast fucking world.

—These boys are on the moving image. Can't get better than these boys.

I looked at the kids and they were videoing each other making star shapes with their arms and legs.

—That the house? said Mick, jerking his head.

—Yeah.

Stevie and the kids practised with their cameras and Mick crossed the quiet road looking right then left. He hunched his shoulders and crouched down with Uncle Septor and Reg. I could see Mick's head going up and down and his trouser arse seam pulling. His trousers were too small or his arse was too big. His jacket rode up to his waist and his boots were turned outwards.

I stood on the edge of the pavement and looked up and down. The road was wide enough to take traffic and cars parked on each side. The pavements were tarmac not slabs. The pavements got soft and tacky in the summer. The cars were parked downhill in front of the garages. The burglar alarm boxes were stuck on the house sides like out-of-reach medicine cupboards. The houses were clean and the grass grew up in fringes around the wallbases like grass round oaks in a kiddy book.

A bird clicked home on heels a road away. A poof preened his prawn horns a house away. A copper's siren played out lonely tom-cat a world away. Mick got up and steadied himself. He looked over and nodded his head. He'd had a haircut and his head was marbled with streaks of skin. He had a long thin plastic bottle of white spirit in his pocket. He undid it with his teeth. He stuffed a strip of old pyjama cloth into it. I started whistling under my breath a tune I'd picked up off the street. The two kids with the video cameras were around me focusing up and Stevie had the tripod out on the roadside. Bertha smelt my leg and lay down with her chin on the floor. I kicked her aside and pushed her along with my reinforced toe and she slid along the tarmac. She got up and walked over to Uncle Septor. Mick cleared his throat, lit up the strip of cloth and went quickly to the front door. He slipped the bottle through the letterbox and jumped back.

—May be a bang, said Stevie.

The kids moved slowly toward the door and stepped back. There was a loud blast as the white spirit caught and the bottle burst. The front door had strips of glass down the side and the hall went red inside. The lounge lit up. The windows were closed. I could smell a burning smell as the front door smoked. I looked away and forced down a lump of phlegm that usually hung around my throat at that time of night. I lifted my head up to make a straight slope for it to run back down. Mick jogged over and told me not to light up near Bertha. She'd got too near the white spirit and caught it on her coat. Stevie got down to the camera viewer and pumped his thumb on the syringe-action attachment that was working the shutter.

The curtain of Hawley's window was set in folds and the

light striped dark and pale. I knew that behind those folds was a fucked-up North Sea fish painting its toenails, working its gills extra fast, crying into its whiskers. Hawley would know what day it was when the door caught and there were only three walls around him. I stood and waited.

Stevie stepped around his tripod and squeezed a small packet of chewing gum tablets. I took two and crushed the candy coats between my back teeth.

—Bloody marvellous, mate. Stevie's face was red and open. Just the smell.

—Smelt it before, said Mick. Used to work the abattoirs. Torching the heads and that. Fucking beautiful.

—Yeah, I said.

—Here you go, kid, put some of them on, why don't you?

Mick handed me a couple of fireworks with Chinese instructions on the cardboard barrel.

—That'll wake him up.

I took the fireworks and crossed to the foot of the tarmac that was Hawley's drive. I wasn't looking at Hawley's window but some things make you look at them even when you don't want to. I was looking straight ahead at Elsa Crippon's gnome cement wishing-well, drawing nicotine from a roll-up clipped to one side of my mouth, thinking of nothing in particular but the unmistakable croon of Karen Carpenter when the curtains moved and I stopped walking. I stood before the door with the noise of the flames crackling through the cheap furniture and the heat of the door smoking and I looked up.

Hawley's face was in between the base of the curtains. He was holding the curtains around his head like a Muslim bird that can't show her hair to the world. He looked like a woman. He looked like a pantomime dame. He looked like he was wearing a scarf that was the size of his window. He was looking down at me from his bowl. His cheeks were wet with crying, his face was stuck like the fish that's got the hook in its mouth and his eyes looked as if something was holding the lids open so he could concentrate on poking them out further. He was pulling the curtains tightly round his head and his hands were going white. He was rocking backwards and forwards against the window. His mouth was going and I knew the shape it was making. 'Lee.' 'Lee.' It was no surprise. His house was burning down and he was in it.

Uncle Septor was on the lawn taking steps around the garden centre ornaments. Reg was twitching in the shade of the weave-slat fence. Mick was swearing over the road with Stevie angling the camera. The kids with the movie cameras were on one knee to shoot from the floor. Under the tripod Bertha was vomiting fish skins. Hawley was scratching from the inside of the window with his thick, long fingernails. He was crying like a baby. The house looked like one person's mistake that had to be corrected quickly from the inside. The flames couldn't live outside. They had to stay behind closed doors like naughty children. The anger would eat itself from inside.

I took a breath and pulled my sweater neck over my mouth. I ran forward and pushed the fireworks through the smoking letter box. It was hot like a heat that you would feel and never remember. It was like Guy Fawkes Night in the park when you didn't get too close because you got burned but your cheeks fired up and you could imagine the flesh going white like cooked chicken. The fireworks were going off in the lounge and the turquoise sparks were jumping around the windows and I stepped back and rocked on my heels and watched Hawley press his jelly nose to the dirty pane of his bowl. 'Help.' Hawley was mouthing a word. That's what

people did when their house was burning down. 'Help.'
That's what they said.

Hawley's little paper dicks would be curling up with the
heat. His long-playing records would be rolling up like
pancakes. He had one of the curtains down around his head.
The flat grey curtain pole was dangling behind his back. I saw
his nightgown. It was soft pink nylon, the type of nylon to go
up in a flash and stick to your skin. I saw down through his
gown to his knees as he leant forward to be saved.

—Hawley, get the fuck down here you little poof! I shouted,
crossly.

I turned away from the cameras.

Hawley started to hold his face and scream. He nodded his
head and sobbed, clutching the curtain around his cheeks.

—Come on. I'm busy. Hurry it up!

I looked at my wrist as if I wore a watch.

Hawley slipped his head out of the curtains. There was a
pause. He came back with the Dansette record player too big
in his arms. He swung it to rest on the window sill and took
it up by its carry handle. He swung the player against the
window and it bounced off, unbalancing him. He came at
the window again and the glass broke.

—Help me, Lee! I'm scared! I heard him screaming from the
window frame.

—Jump, I shouted.

I stood with my back to him.

—I can't! I'm scared!

I started to walk away. Uncle Septor and Reg were back in
the shade dancing about. Mick was over the road and he had
his finger poking at my collarbone.

—What do you think you're doing?

He pushed his head into my face.

—Get off me.

—You're for it.

I pushed my wet eyes into Mick's nostrils and breathed the rank hygiene from his bad teeth. He took his finger off. I heard Hawley whine.

—I can't do it, Lee!

I moved back to the window and held my arms out as if he was going to throw a small light parcel down. He put one leg over the window and swung so he was straddling the frame.

—Ooh, it's too painful, he cried. He swung the other leg over so he was sitting on the frame. I could see the room going red and his face getting sweaty.

—I think I've got smoke inhalation! My nightie's going to catch!

—You're a dead homosexual. Mick lunged at me.

—I'VE SEEN THE FUCKER CRY.

I started running backwards and forwards under the window with my arms outspread. Hawley slipped so he was hanging on to the frame by his hands and elbows. He lowered down and closed his eyes. He let go with his hands and came down through the air like misshapen lead rain. His nightgown flared out like the skirts of a jellyfish. His tight shiny plastic pants flashed. I let him fall and went to pick him up.

—We'll take it from here.

I heard Uncle Septor's voice behind me and felt his arm on my back. His hand was thin like a claw. I stood over Hawley and the fireworks blasted colour chips around the shell of the cardboard house like multicoloured fireballs.

—All right, son.

There was a new voice. I looked around. It was DC Marcus Serpell. I coughed with the feeling I was turning into water.

13. I'm Hanging Off the Stair Rail

I'm hanging off the stair rail. I'm leaning backwards and holding on to the top of the stairs with both hands. I'm swinging my body out over the stairwell so they will find me at the bottom when I slip and fall on my head. I'm humming so that my head vibrates inside and I can't see properly.

I'm humming the noise of the cars on the main road when they go past fast and the old dear takes my wrist and pulls me closer so that I lean out from her too because I don't like her so close. I'm humming the hymn from the nativity where Joseph lays the baby onto the strips of paper and the angels stand around and look on and where Mary sings on her own about once in Royal David's city except no-one can hear because she's too quiet and the toddlers come on in sheep outfits with white tights and leotards for the boys too. I'm humming the song that Mary sings when she's got her new baby and it's going to save the world. And it's special because it's born in a manger where the animals eat and it gets a capital letter even when you don't use its name. And He will grow up and make dead men walk around and blind people see and He will give dinner to the starving and it'll be bread. And He will bring fishes out of the canals. And His name will be Little Chubby Junior of the Surrey Housing Estate.

The wood is varnished so thickly that my hands are slipping unless I cling on tight. I'm using the stair rail to hold me up and I'm leaning back and I know it will never break and I will never fall. I'm putting both feet against the step and I'm locking my arms and my hair is standing straight off my head. That's what I do. When the dark hasn't come yet and the old dear's told me not to go downstairs again. I put one bare foot on top of the other and stand falling over except for the stair rail. I look down the stairs and hear the newsreader and catch my old man clearing his throat and saying something to her. And I bend my body down around to the first step as if I am hanging off a building and I sing out loudly the songs of the adverts or the hymns of the nativity or the tune of the cop show where the two men drive around in a low red car that can't open its doors so the cops have to climb in through the window, where the dark cop cries and the blond one sits in a big wicker chair and plays the guitar.

The old man shouts from the settee 'get upstairs' and I run across the landing and jump on to my bed so I land on my knees and I pull the sheets off the bed and get in from the bottom and I wait so he can come up. And then I get out and go to the stair rail again and I hang off so I think my head is going to touch the carpet from bending backwards and I can feel my backbone bending like a bow but I lean back all the same. And then the old dear comes up the stairs and shakes her hands in front of her so I will go where her hands are shaking and that is my bedroom and she holds the sheets open until I get in and I kick at her legs where she is standing and she moves them and I say that I want the old man not her and she pushes my hair off my forehead and says he is tired with digging up the road and I say I want him and I try to slip down between the wall and the bed to get away from her and he never comes up and sometimes I cry out loud so he will hear me.

I go into the bathroom so the lino's cold on my white feet and I pull my pyjama trousers down so I can walk along on the material. I put both arms along the sink and look in the mirror. I take the old man's purple-handle razor and put it on my cheek and make the movement that the old man makes when he is getting rid of the hairs off his chin. I haven't got any hairs on my chin. I pull the razor across my jaw and feel the skin with the palm of my hand like the old man does. And I try it on the back of my hand and there are no hairs there either so I pull my trouser leg up and run the razor up from my ankle to my knee but I do it too fast because the blade catches on the skin and cuts off a small piece of flesh so there is blood running down towards my foot and I shake my leg. I sit on the crapper and peel off the bathroom roll and lick the cheap paper and stick it over the blood and I watch the blood get bigger on the paper. And I take the paper off and look at the place and it's white where the skin has gone. The blood dries on my leg and I scrape it off and put it on the crapper lid. I roll my trouser leg down and step out to the top of the landing and I look down at the light that's coming from the lounge and I step down on to the first step and wait. I wait and I hear the weatherman say 'rain in some parts' and I step down again and stand on tiptoes holding my breath. I walk down the stairs and stand in the hall and listen. I go into the kitchen and open the back door as slowly as I know will make no sound and I step outside on to the cold pale concrete step and on to the moss of the patio.

The grass is wet with night-time water so I hop over and snake around the side of the house. There are no plants in our garden. My old man uses the weedkiller all year round. He says he doesn't want the work. That's why the grass grows like the hair of seventy different old men. It's long, short, thick, thin and bald under the whirligig washing line where the old dear's shoes stamp the life out. There is a plant coming out of the wall at the side of the house and it's green all year round and it catches me when I try and get round and it holds me by the pyjama pocket like a relative that wants kissing and I swear my swear words and pull away.

There's no-one out here. The birds are indoors wrapping up their youngsters for happy dreams and the blokes are getting in their first rounds. No-one's looking out through the grey lacy curtains of their homes. The ground is cold and wet under my feet and there are smooth bits and sharp bits of the road and I walk along the tarmac where it's soft and I stand on the white lines because they can't hurt you and then I hold my weight off my feet and walk carefully over the pebbly park entrance and I'm under the street light and I'm in my pyjamas.

The park's wet like it's been washed. It looks the way the kitchen table looks when the old dear's had her cloths over it and you can see the water slicks by bending down in the light. The park is fresh like vegetables washed before you have to use them. The water is up my pyjama leg. I'm wearing flares. I'm wearing eight-year-old's pyjamas and I don't have the waist to hold them up. I stand between the concrete posts and then I jump my waist on to the middle post so my legs are off the ground and I run over to the swings in the cold and I stand up on the kiddy swing and start to swing by pressing down on my knees as if I'm a mechanical contraption that is going faster and faster.

They're building the Red Indian lookout. There's a little bulldozer with a forklift attachment parked facing the dug-up soil. There are little lumps of earth. There is a ring like a circus ring where the council telegraph poles will go. There are holes where the council telegraph poles will go. The ring is roped off with shiny plastic strips tied to thin metal posts but the kids go all over the soil digging their castles and cities that will last until morning. The soil is flat now and there is a rim where you can see how deep the grass grows on the earth and it's not very deep and there are no roots and the soil changes colour so it's light underneath.

I'm standing on the red plastic swing and I've got my head back so far that I am pushing faster and faster on my legs and I am going higher and higher and I am looking at the brown soil scar that's in the middle of the park where the castle was in a different time. It's cold, so cold on my soft easy-bruise skin and my pyjamas are dampening up in the night water and my toes are curling up on the swing grooves and I am singing so loudly the hymn where Joseph puts the baby in the strips of paper where the animals eat and I am singing the words over and over again and no-one is coming and the soil is flat like someone's been there smoothing it out and all the little cities have gone and the lamps are standing around the park like tall skinny people that are employed only for their bright orange heads and it's misty in the park from all the washing that's made it so fresh and it's dark in the corners and I am going to walk in the soil.

I stand on the swing and bend my knees to slow down the swing as if it's a horse and I'm on Saturday morning ranch adventure television. I wait for the swing to slow and it does and I slip off into the grass and jump up when I feel the blades slipping up over my feet. I run over to the plastic strips of the little building site and put my hands on the ground to crawl under. Now I'm in the ring of the soil and I'm running around and I start to run round again and again until I can see my prints growing like fork marks in the butter and I keep on going and then I get tired and lie down on the earth and look up at the mist and think it's hard to be here where there are no clues.

There is the sound of a night walker clearing his throat and there is a dog clipping on the pathway. A lighter is fuelling a fag and the links of the dog chains are touching each other in a man's hand and I lie still until the man shouts my name 'LEE TREBILCOCK IN PYJAMAS' and I get up and run to the park entrance and past the posts that keep the cars out. I hop around my house to the back door where I open so slowly that no-one hears and I creep on tiptoes back up the stairs and crawl up through the bed with my heart beating so fast I put my hand on my chest and think that I will have a heart attack and they'll know where I've been. And I lie still on my back with my head turned to the cartoon car wallpaper and I watch the pictures while my heart is beating and I cross my hands over my chest so I will be in the right position for the coffin and I stop panting and begin to feel sleepy and I curl up into a ball towards the wallpaper and I hear the old dear coming up the stairs and she's pushing my door across the carpet and she comes up to the bed and I stay still like I'm dead and she doesn't feel my chest to see if I'm still alive and I don't turn over and then I'm tired and I rub my toes together to comfort me from her.

When I was a kid I broke into houses. I broke windows and stood on water tanks and climbed in through rusty window frames and poked around the old people's things and took what I liked. I took a biro with J P W written on the body and a self-timing parking keyring that ticked when you set it and went off in your pocket when your time was up. I had photos away and I put them on the flower beds in the park so the old ones would see them on their way through the grass. I got in all the gardens and pulled up the fruits and ate them in the street. I wore little canvas baseball boots decorated like the American flag and jeans that dragged on the floor. I wore easy sweatshirts and singlets. You'd find me on the bench outside Chubby's, draining a see-through can of cola, looking through the plastic to see how far there was to go, kicking both legs in a rhythm that was waiting for something to happen.

I hung around the Leisure Lounge banging the machines for ten pees. The other kids changed them up for twos and ones and put them in the penny pushing machine where the long arm pushed the coppers towards the edge and dropped them down into the slot only they never dropped because the man who invented the machine was clever. I waited and watched the boys on the fruit machines and I put my ten pence in when I knew it was going to happen and it didn't pay off but I played the real game. I picked up the fag butts off the floor and unpeeled the brown tips and pulled the brown cotton wool filters apart and threw them back down. I didn't know how to smoke but I used the old man's lighter when it was on top of his fags in the lounge and he was at the door. The old man always had the cleaning demonstrators in. He said it was a nasty job foaming the carpets and someone had to do it but he never bought any of it. I'd be sitting on the settee edge on tiptoes clicking his lighter on and off listening to the gas wheeze while the flame burned low in the sky-blue plastic.

I went over to my Aunt Margot and kissed the cat so it ran off and got run over and we found it on the way to Chubby's with its arms folded in the gutter with number plate chips where the driver had pulled it off the car. Aunt Margot pushed me on to her tit and held me close and told me to smooth her down but I didn't. I was six. I knew what tits were for and that was baby's milk.

When I was a kid I got through to the operator on the public phone ten or twelve times a day and told her to fuck off until the coppers came down our road asking if the kids were using the phone.

When I was a kid the primary school doctor told me to wear corrective glasses and an eye patch but I wasn't standing around in the playground with the hard ones looking like that. I'd sooner have a squint but I never did and I never grew up short-sighted.

We were having fish bites. My old dear liked to buy the big bags of fish food from the ice supermarket and the old man ran her down there once a week so she could get the big bottles of vegetable oil and bags of chips and chicken nuggets and cod pieces. At half past five every evening except for Sundays she got out the saucepan which had the oil and chip basket in and she put the electric heat on under it and she sat down at the kitchen picnic table and read the local paper while the old man sat in front of the national news so he could swear at it.

We were having fish bites and the old dear was over the paper on her elbows and the oil was getting bigger in the saucepan so there was black around the edges and the fish bites were propped against the wall ready to go in and the chips were in the basket clipped away from the oil and the oil was creeping up to get at the chips like little dragons and the old man was on the settee so I could see his vest through his shirt. I liked fish bites. I made the old dear cook them so I could line them up on my plate in order of size starting with the smallest. The old dear was looking at the pictures in the newspaper and the old man was swearing at the news where the grey woman politician was turning into a man and I was on the settee with my feet flat on the vinyl pushing under the old man's leg. I was jiggling my feet under the old man's leg and he was telling me to stop. I'd been in the bath with my wind-up yellow octopus that swum along and I'd been making island countries out of the bubble-bath bubbles and I'd had the flannel wet over my face until I had to stop because I couldn't breathe and I'd been singing the adverts. The old dear had me in pyjamas and a big boy's nappy because I didn't have the control yet for night-times and we didn't have that many sheets for change. I was handling the old man's throwaway lighter that was sky-blue and I was trying to click it on and the old man was snatching it away and I was jiggling my feet under his leg and he was pushing me away. The fish bites were on and there was no news and I was talking in a special language that I didn't understand and I wanted the old man to be proud of me and the old man was smoking on his cigarettes and it was light outside.

The old man was stretching his arms so his hands went across my face and I was laughing and I was pulling on his arm and he was shaking it away from me and the old dear was speaking through the hatch and the old man was pulling his body to the edge of the settee and I was patting his pockets. Got to nip down the road, the old man was saying, and he was standing up and he was putting his hand in his pocket and he was taking out his money of fifty pences and tens and twenties and he was picking up the cardboard of the fag packet and he was squeezing the cardboard together and I was holding his lighter. Give me that then, the old man was pointing at the lighter and I was clinging to it with my hand so it was hidden and he had my hand and he was undoing the fingers and I was doing them back up and he was shouting and I was giving him the lighter and he was saying he was only going to get his fags and I could have ten pence for school and I was standing up and taking the money and I had it in my pyjama pocket and the old man was scratching his head where he'd sweated and he was doing up his flies and he was shouting through the hatch to the old dear but the old dear was busy with the fish bites and she wasn't lifting her head and I was listening to the front door open and counting the time it took for the door to shut because I knew the count of that just like I knew the count between the rings of the telephone and that was six. The old man always slammed the door and I watched his shape go past and then I lay along the settee on my back and I arched my body up so my chin was stuck on my chest and I shouted at the old dear with a voice like I was being strangled but she just went on with the fish bites and I kicked the vinyl cushions off the settee so they were on the floor and I pulled them back up without touching the floor and I rearranged them and lay back down and arched my back so my little groin was in the air and I lay back down and watched the screen of the news but I wasn't watching the news and the fish bites were ready and I heard the sauce and vinegar bottles go on to the table and the old dear had her head out of the hatch shouting for Frank and Frank wasn't there. And I went upstairs and got the razor down out of the cup shaped into a sperm whale and I used the blade on the polystyrene wallpaper so there were cuts and I had my toe on the little Ferrari car and I was driving the little car with my toe into the dips of the carpet and I was playing quietly so the old dear would love me and the old man would come back.

Uncle Septor was coming over because no-one knew where the old man was and the old dear couldn't leave me and they said they hadn't seen the old man up at the shop and Uncle Septor was going down to the club and up to Chubby's and he was asking up and down the street if they'd seen Frank and Uncle Septor was in the lounge on the settee where Frank sat and Uncle Septor was looking stern and the old dear was looking older. It was getting dark and Majollica was taking me upstairs and I was holding on to the stair rail with both hands and I wasn't going and I was screaming and kicking and biting and I could smell Majollica's dentures and I could see the sticky crumbs in her overall pocket. I was biting Majollica's wrist and she was pulling her hand away and I was running upstairs and I had the sheets up over my head and I was lying in a ball on my knees and shouting and the old dear was by the bed and I was on my side kicking the old dear fast at the knees and she was bending over and moving her top nearer my face and her legs way from my legs and she was saying 'sorry'. And I was screaming into her face and Uncle Septor was at the bottom of the stairs saying he'd be back tomorrow to see the coppers and that he had things he had to do. The old dear was starting to cry and I was screaming louder when I saw the tears and I was ripping in half and the old dear was crumbling and Uncle Septor had things he had to do.

Uncle Septor brought over poster pictures of the old man from the copy shop and a pair of coppers came round and asked the old dear if there'd been any trouble and the old dear was telling them about the fish bites and I was on the stairs running the cars over my palms and Majollica was in the kitchen with the stainless steel kettle. The copper was holding Uncle Septor's poster and the old man's head was folded into four pieces and he was wearing his green hat that folded down over his ears when it was cold only he never folded the monkey ears down and his face looked dead. I was on the floor by the fireside tearing up a sew-by-number embroidery card of a pair of lambs from Majollica's country cottage sewing basket and it was to take my mind off things because it was the day after but the fish bites were under the washing line and Uncle Septor was all over the settee.

I'm lying with my back flat on the bed and my legs against the wall so they prop on the window sill and I'm doing the back-straightening exercises they tell us about in school and I'm kicking at my Goofy night light with one foot and I'm pulling my stomach apart with my hands so I won't ever have to go downstairs and see her again and she's been up here and she's been kissing me but she can't talk properly and Majollica's moved in from over the road. And the posters of my old man have been up as far as the roundabout and no-one's seen anything and they've finished the Red Indian lookout but I'm not looking out and there's only earth where there used to be grass and how many real Red Indians live on the Surrey Housing Estate anyway.

14. Home

Alun Glenhusky was on the poof. He was wearing a dark suit and a tight white shirt. As he turned his legs the shirt opened and I could see grey belly hair through the gap. His tie fell forward and his shoes were pointing in opposite directions. Majollica's bottle of Tio Pepe sherry was on the mantelpiece. The old dear and Majollica were in the kitchen putting the plates away.

I was on the settee with my legs apart looking straight ahead. I was wearing black trousers which picked up a turquoise fleck and a black jacket with gold buttons. I was wearing a wide tie made of silk orange and green circles. I was lighting a Fabulously Regal and I was squeezing the end so the cigarette was flat and I was sucking my cheeksides to get the nicotine in. Glenhusky was looking at me and then down at his feet. I was looking at the haywain above his head.

I had styling product in my hair so my fringe stayed off my face and my sideboards were slicked to my jawline. I was in scaffold rubber-sole loafers and thin black socks that made my ankles look slim. I was pulling hot cigarette tip over the old ash of the ashtray in my hand and I could feel heat in my palm.

Majollica walked through from the kitchen into the lounge and leaned against Glenhusky to take his sherry glass. Glenhusky looked up at her and nodded as she held the glass up to ask if he'd finished. I looked away. Majollica went out again.

I stood up and shook one leg and then the other so my trouser legs wouldn't catch around my knees or in my shoe sides. I set my jacket fronts together. I cleared my throat and stepped out to the stairs. I took hold of the stair post and pulled myself up the bare wood stairs. I was going into the crapper.

I stood against the porcelain sink and turned on the overhead light strip and put my face up close to the glass. I stretched my cheeks and looked in at the wide pores. I licked my palm and smoothed down my sideboards and turned my head so that my eyes stayed looking at themselves and I watched my hair fold back on itself to make a small oatmeal quiff.

I snapped the light off and walked into my bedroom. The pictures of the birds were gone and the wall was marked with little circles where the fasteners had been. There was a picture of the Chivermouth Forefathers lining up with a football under their own biro signatures. My Goofy night light was unplugged and the flex wrapped around the tail and ears on the window sill. My bedside Awakener said 2.35 p.m.

Hawley was on the bed under the sheets with his hands crossed over his chest. His face was white and his hair was soft and shapeless around his temples. His nose was squashy and his fleshy mouth was open.

I sat down on the side of the single bed and put one hand on his thigh. I left my hand there and leaned under the bed. I came back up with a small magazine in my other hand. I opened up the magazine and propped it up while I found the page. I licked one finger and pulled the pages towards me. I found the page and looked at the picture.

—This bloke gets it when he goes into a bookshop, I said to Hawley but Hawley didn't move his head.

—Fucking brilliant this one, I said again. Bird gets up a ladder and you can see it all. He's after his fucking encyclopaedia and that. You know what it's all about, mate.

I looked out of the window. All I could see was the sky and it was grey in streaks like layers so soon there would be no sun.

Hawley moved his leg.

I looked down at him and moved my hand.

—All right, mate?

—Yes, he said.

—What about a bit of tomato soup for you? Nice tomato soup? Good for you!

—Oh thanks, Lee.

—Tomato soup for Hawley! I told Majollica. He's awake. I've got to step out for a while.

I looked in at Glenhusky and then turned and stepped out of the house. I slammed the door after me and stood on the front step. I lifted my jacket fronts and put my hands in my trouser pockets and started to walk towards the park.

The trees were beginning to grow their spring leaves and they were making an arc over the concrete posts. I passed through watching the ground. I followed the tarmac path and walked quickly towards the bouncy chickens and beyond where a little yellow digger was idling and two men were crouching with hard hats. I walked over to little metal posts and stood against plastic sashes. They were digging up the Red Indian lookout.

The men saw me and looked up. They stood up and held their collars away from their necks and got back down again. I looked down and kicked at the loosened sods.

The kids were on the swings like noisy birds that don't know what was going on. They shouted at me and I kept my back to them. I made prints of my loafers in the earth and walked around the posts until I was at the other side of the lookout and I could see the council telegraph poles lying on top of each other like a pile of lumber. The poles were green and they had dark brown ends where they'd been in the earth. I walked on further and went to sit on one of the benches where the old ones sat about watching the dogs on leads. I sat down and watched the men.

Uncle Septor was on remand awaiting the Crown Court for attempted murder, rape and racial attack. We'd been to the magistrate's committal. Reg, Mick and Stevie were in with him. They'd let me go. They said I was defending Hawley and that there was insufficient evidence to prosecute for the student kid in The King's Limb seeing as Uncle Septor had admitted to rogering the kid unprotected in one of the crapper booths. The coppers didn't know it all. Uncle Septor hadn't told it all. All we knew was that they were digging up the Red Indian lookout and there was new evidence to suggest Uncle Septor knew more about my old man's disappearance than he had said.

I hadn't been to work. Ronald said I needed time off to sort things out and that they were all behind me. Even Lorraine. And Little Chubby Junior was sending down battered skate every day with Delia.

The men were stopping for lunch. One of them was getting into the cab of the digger and the other was leaning against the cab door. They were opening ice-cream boxes of sandwiches and unscrewing grubby flasks so they could pour tea into plastic cup tops. I looked away.

They'd found a lighter. A dirty, blue, rusted, disposable lighter, clogged up with earth so it would never work again. They found it around the edge of the earth circle and now the digger was carefully pulling up soil around the middle and the men were digging by hand.

DC Serpell had been round to the house. He hadn't sat down. He said they'd opened an investigation and they'd be talking to us. He said they would get to the bottom of it and that they had their men on it and the old dear had sat smiling and shaking on the poof and Alun Glenhusky had stood behind her with his arm on her shoulder and Majollica had been in the kitchen with the stainless steel teapot.

Uncle Septor had written me a letter on reporter's notebook paper folded into a copper's envelope. I hadn't read it but I'd held it up to the light. Nobody ever wrote letters to me. I'd put the letter away. I'd always struggled with people's writing. I was all right with the printed word.

Sitting on the bench, I took the envelope out from my inside breast pocket. I slid my finger into the envelope back and ripped the paper open. The words were long and spidery like Uncle Septor's legs. They said 'Dear son'.

Letter From Uncle Septor

Dear son.

I read as the men sipped at their warm tea and looked straight ahead and thought about what they would be finding that afternoon.

They've got me in here now. They've got Reginald and Mick and Stevie. It's up to you now. You know what to do. Carry it on, Lee. The boys will look up to you. Don't look at me when they get me in the court. Got to keep the strength. Got to fight it.

Never regret. Never look back. You've got the keys to the trike. They might let you live on in the house. The curtains are under the sink. You'll find them.

They're saying things about me and Frank but you mustn't listen to them. I loved my brother. We had an argument, son, and I knocked the old bastard out. You'll know which way to think. Your dad was for my Brenda and her darkie boyfriend. He was telling me to get out of it. Said I was no good. Well, I showed him didn't I? Eh, Lee? Put him under the playpark, didn't I?

Don't tell the cops anything. Let them work it out. I'm going to be away for a while now. Look after the trike. I'll need that when I get out of here.

Remember, son. Never regret.

Your Uncle Septor.

I folded up the letter and put it back in the envelope.

The old dear was red in the face when I got back.

—They've found him, haven't they?

—No.

—It's been days now. They'll find him. I know it.

Glenhusky was upstairs with Hawley and the old dear was at the sink with her apron.

—Got to clean things up, she said.

I went to get the door before 'Auld Lang Syne' played out.

DC Serpell and WPC Marina Sprott were on the step with their heads turned to one side.

—All right, lad? asked Serpell.

—Yeah, I said, stepping out, closing the front door behind me.

—You look shaken, said WPC Sprott and she took my hand and rubbed it with hers. I took my hand away.

—The old dear's OK.

—Good. They're pretty sure he's down there somewhere. Your Uncle Septor said he was up late that night with things to do. We're getting somewhere.

Serpell chewed at his nails.

—And they found your dad's lighter! said Sprott.

—Yeah, I said. I threw it away.

—Oh!

—It didn't work any more.

—You poor boy!

—How's young Hawley Harvey Crippon? asked Serpell.

—He's upstairs. He's OK. He's going to London with Alun Glenhusky to live with them and their new twins. He's all right. How's that student kid anyway?

—Michael McCarthy?

—Whatever.

—Out of danger and on his way home. He'll be back at the university next year.

—Oh. Great.

It was over. I said I'd see them again and started to walk away, over the road, to Chubby's, anywhere. The panda started up. I followed it slowly up the road like a dog that knows it's got to chase but not why.

The panda turned out of the road and I walked on passing Richard and Majollica's where the folded chairs were leaning against the guttering on the uneven grass, past Uncle Septor's where the milk bottles were empty and forgotten on the tunnel step, past the houses covered inside with lacy curtains and outside with crapper overflow stain.

I reached the corner of the cul-de-sac and smelt Little Chubby Junior frying up the lunches for the Surrey Housing Estate. I thought of turkey on a stick.

I stopped when I saw a shape covering the cartoon cod OPEN CLOSED sign.

The shape was against the glass and it was holding itself up with its hands deep in silk bomber jacket pockets. The shape was looking down. It looked like it was crying.

—Deborah! I cried.

Deborah's shoulders jumped. She looked round as far as she could and took in some air through her teeth.

—It's me, I said.

I stood there, feet flat in loafers, knees pushed back making my trousers wrinkle and flare out over my shins, belt pushing the material into ridges. My shirt was misshapen and my hands were forcing my trousers down below my waist. My jacket bagged over my chest. My neck started where the shirt stopped. It was brown and thick and made stronger by the cream and ginger check colours. My chin was shaven and smooth. My eyes were dark like thick tubes for endless journeys. My forehead was a bit wrinkled. I could feel it. My hair was washed and set. I was Deborah's if she wanted me, all-singing, all-dancing, all-sorry for fucking her in the Red Indian lookout when she wasn't looking out.

—You look awful. What's happened?

—Nothing. How did you find me?

—I looked. Are you sure there's nothing wrong?

—Yeah. Wanted to see you. Been thinking. That night.

—Yes?

I turned my shoe over.

—I'm, er, sorry. Yeah?

—Oh.

—What happened and that. Got out of control.

—It's all right. I mean, I understand. I think. I did think you liked me.

Deborah went red and that was a lot of red for one face in the pale sunlight from the window on to the sky.

—I do.

—Really?

—'Course. D'you think I'm like that with all the birds?

She laughed and spat little saliva balls over her fingers.

I walked round so I was standing right in front of her.

—Why don't you stand up then or are you stuck there on your arse?

Deborah moved from where she'd been leaning against the glass. I stepped back. She approached. I put both hands on her shoulders and turned my head close to her face. I leant forward and looked at her lips, placing mine over them and pressing. I watched her eyes close and moved my face so her lips would open. I side-stepped to turn my chin upwards. Her lips opened and I moved my tongue to the front of my mouth. I touched her tongue with mine and we felt the electricity of pulling your jumper over your head in the dark when the sparks fly and crackle round your ears.

It was quiet all around us as we spun like turntables against the grey sky, pushing our tongues deeper inside each other, reaching for the next bit to hold on to when we'd linked hands then arms then bodies.

We kissed with no more than space between us. I stopped and pulled my mouth away to look at Deborah's eyes. She was crying a bit.

—What's wrong?

I laughed. I didn't want to but I did. She was a funny bird. She stood away.

—What's going to happen?

—What d'you mean?

—I'm carrying Cedar's baby. And your uncle. And everything.

—What about you and your Cedar then?

—He's all right. He's getting better. We weren't very close. I
mean he liked rock pools and that sort of thing. And I don't.
We were quite casual. I thought I loved him but that was just
because he showed me some attention. He doesn't know
about the baby. I'll tell him.

—Best way.

—Yes.

—Then we can get organized with a home for it and that.

—Oh yes.

—A little Lebanese chap then.

—We can have more.

—Yeah, love.

I held on to her fingers. I liked Deborah.

—Deborah, do you fancy meeting my old dear? She's a bit
confused.

—Yes, Lee, I would.

—Fucking weird, isn't it?

—Yes.

—You and me.

—Yes.

—I like thin blondes.

—Do you think it will all be all right?

—Yeah. Give us your number then.

I took the bird's number and started back down my road.